GET WITCH QUICK

A WILDES WITCHES MYSTERY BOOK 9

MARA WEBB

1

"Quin, I have another complaint letter here," I huffed. I gave my cat a curious glare as he swaggered into the room, sometimes it was fun to guess what excuse he might come up with this time. He jumped up the bottom few steps of the staircase and watched me read out the letter that had just been pushed under the door.

"Dear Ms. Wildes,

It is my regret to inform you that, once again, your cat endangered the lives of employees of the sanitation department of Sucré. I'm sure that you do not need to be reminded that this is the third letter that I have sent. I appreciate that cats are hard to train, but this cannot continue. If there is a fourth incident, then I will have no choice but to remove your address from the route for garbage collection."

"Let me stop you there," Quin began. "I still don't see how I am 'endangering lives', surely what I am doing is something that they train for."

"Sorry, you think that a cat trying to climb into the back of the garbage truck, the area with all the moving parts, isn't dangerous? They don't know that you have magic powers to keep yourself safe!

They have been diving into the back to pull you out and they are going to stop picking up our trash if you do it again!" I exclaimed.

"Nora, come on, you know as well as I do that there is a cover up in this town and I'm not planning to just look the other way!" he howled, galloping away up the stairs to add a dramatic flair to his argument.

If there was someone on the cusp of inheriting magical powers from a witch, like I had done, then I would feel compelled to warn them that the hardest part, by far, is dealing with your talking cat. He tests my patience hourly, but his latest obsession is going to be the final straw.

Quin was the owner of a café in town, *The Catmosphere Café*, but had taken some time off to catch up on some TV shows he had recorded. I knew straight away that this would be problematic when I saw the names of his shows. 'Caught in the act', 'Red handed; red knife', and 'Law-abiding paws' to list a few. He was about to go deep into a fantasy land where everyone he saw was a master criminal.

The show 'law-abiding paws' was all about the sniffer dogs that the police employ, he claimed to have only recorded this to make fun of dogs that were stupid enough to get jobs when they could just get fed for free by a human, but then he got hooked on a story line about money laundering and it's all he's talked about since.

He had convinced himself, based on no evidence, that the staff that travel with the garbage truck were smuggling money from one bad guy to the next. He wanted to hide in the back of the truck and catch them in the act of fishing out a garbage bag full of cash and leave it for someone to find.

It wasn't the worst way to move money around, I guess. No one would question those guys collecting trash bags, so money could get collected, then if they tucked it somewhere easy to grab, I suppose they could pull it back out and hand it to their mafia boss. Clearly, I had spent too much time giving Quin's ideas consideration and needed to speak to a normal person.

As if he could hear my silent plea for help, my boyfriend stepped through the front door of my house. Ryan was not only gorgeous, kind, on the magical high-council with me, and the most wonderful person I knew, but he was also a lawyer. If I got into a sticky situation over this garbage truck incident then he might be able to help me.

Before I had the chance to show him the letter, he wrapped his hand around my body and pulled me into his chest so he could kiss me. All concerns about Quin left me temporarily as I closed my eyes and pressed my mouth to Ryan's. I didn't open my eyes again until he started speaking.

"You look how I feel," he sighed.

"Tough day?" I asked.

"Tough week," he replied. "I'm being roped in on some huge legal action against a company selling 'wellness shakes' and I am being totally buried in paperwork. Apparently they have been telling their valued customers that the nutritional content contributes to glossy hair, weight loss, perfect skin and some other nonsense. The people complaining have not achieved the advertised results, let's put it that way."

He was holding his briefcase and the fastenings looked like they were about to burst open. Ever since I'd seen a vision of our wedding day, I'd been expecting that he could propose at any moment. I hadn't mentioned it to him, and I certainly hadn't told Quin as he would have told Ryan immediately. I wanted it to happen organically, but I sort of hoped he would pop the question sooner rather than later.

He put the briefcase down, kicked off his shoes and shuffled towards the sofa before collapsing onto it. My house was more central in Sucré than his, so with his increased work load he had been spending most nights here instead of driving back and forth from his place. We were pretty much living together full time now, I couldn't even remember when we had last slept apart.

"I was planning to make stew," I said. "Don't know why I said I was *planning* it, it's already in the slow cooker."

"Sounds good," he mumbled through a pillow. With the deepest part of winter behind us, I was ready for spring. Just because I felt ready, it didn't mean the weather had picked up. It was as cold now as it had been four weeks ago and I had been busting out my winter cookbooks every night to find creative ways to warm us up from the inside out.

"I recommend the chili," Edith hollered from the hallway mirror. My aunt was dead but, due to the fact that she was a witch, was able to appear to me as a ghost in the mirrors of the house that I had inherited from her.

A cookbook appeared on the kitchen counter that I hadn't seen before, she must have transported it down from the attic library. The hardback cover opened and the pages began to flip over so quickly that it was almost a blur, finally settling on a recipe that was accompanied with a photograph of oven glove-wearing hands holding a pot of the most incredible food. Sold. I could freeze the stew once it was done and eat it another day.

I set about preparing the vegetables, pre-heating pans and stirring while Ryan snored away from the living room. It would take at least forty minutes once everything was bubbling together, it already smelled heavenly, but I could take care of some other business while I waited.

"Devoco," I commanded, holding out my hand as my laptop came flying into the room and landed on my palm. I sat at the breakfast bar and opened up my computer to check my emails. I had sent my O.W.L. tutor a query and was hoping that she had responded.

Since I hadn't been raised by the magical community, Edith had enrolled me into O.W.L., the Online Witch Learning school. This program was designed to teach me everything that I would need to function as a witch out in the world. I had learned the basics of my powers, how to defend myself, how to counteract poisons and now I was being set my hardest task yet.

I was close to graduating, it was to be expected that they would make things more challenging, but this was something else. This assignment relied on Quin and I working together, we had to fuse our thoughts, think as one, and complete an assault course blindfolded. Well, I would be the one blindfolded, Quin would be stood on the sidelines giving me directions such as when to jump, climb or duck.

The assault course would also be lined with dangers of the magical variety and Quin would need to tell me how to get to the end safely. I was certain that this activity would be the death of me. My tutor, Professor Eastey, had sent over a collection of bonding exercises to help Quin and I work together. I had expressed my concern that Quin wasn't known for his ability to concentrate, deliver succinct sentences or think of people other than himself.

Her reply was not reassuring, *'Cats will be cats, good luck!'.*

"Quin!" I called. No response. Yeah, he was going to get me killed. I read through the list that my tutor had sent, I spotted an activity called 'memory wall' and it seemed like the least awful of her suggestions.

We would choose an area of the house and work together to cover that wall in memories from our lives before we were connected. Quin had been my aunt's familiar, and I had lived a human life in another town. I had been married and divorced, worked crummy jobs to make ends meet and then had my world turned around by inheriting powers, a house, and a talking cat.

We had briefly mentioned things from the past to each other, but this seemed like a sweet way to build on that. Besides, I needed to do everything I could to ensure my survival on this bonding assault course otherwise I would plummet off a high platform or get shot at by a bow and arrow.

I began to cook the rice, setting out dishes on the dining table and considering when would be a good time to wake up my boyfriend. I figured he would want to get a drink for himself, so I would go and get him now. A spluttering engine outside made me jump and was also enough to cause Ryan to lurch onto his feet.

It sounded like an old scooter, almost as if an Italian vespa from a grey-scale movie was driving down the street. It backfired once or twice more before silence was restored. "Hey, dinner is nearly ready," I smiled. Ryan rubbed at his eyes and then checked his watch.

"Sorry, I've been totally floored at work today, I'm not great company," he grumbled. "I'll just go grab a t-shirt, if I get food on this shirt *again* this week I think it will tip me over the edge."

He went upstairs to rummage through the section of the closet that I had cleared for him to use. With him spending more time here, and me spending time at his place, we had started to leave things around. I had a spare toothbrush and a hairdryer at his house, but he had moved at least half of his wardrobe here.

I heard a strange clicking, like high heels on stone. Tap-tap. Then a knock at the front door. "Don't look at me," Quin muttered as he trotted into the kitchen. Clearly, he thought nothing of invading date night. The knock rang out again, so I crossed the hallway and pulled open the door.

Standing at the top of the steps leading up to my house was a woman that, without heels, would have been only slightly shorter than me. Her heels gave her the height advantage, and I was able to see her brown hair neatly pulled into a side bun underneath a large hat. The moped I had heard was parked beside my car, had she driven here on that thing in a sun hat?

"Nora," she smiled, stretching her arms out wide and wrapping them around me tightly. I didn't know how to respond. Ryan jogged down the stairs behind me and I heard him stop as he tried to make sense of what he was seeing.

"Ryan, this is my mother," I explained. I had no idea what she was doing here.

2

"Hello Mrs. Wildes. It's a pleasure to meet you," Ryan said, reaching out for a handshake like he was at a business meeting.

"It's not Wildes, it's Jackson," I muttered out of the corner of my mouth. Ryan gave a small nod of acknowledgment as he remembered that my mom had changed her last name after she married my stepdad, I had kept Wildes.

"About that," she sighed, stepped back to look at us both. "I think I will take Wildes back after all." I gave her a puzzled brow.

"Wildes is your dad's name, why would you take that back?" I asked.

"I just like it. Lee and I have had another argument and I thought this might light a fire under him," she grinned. If there was anyone on earth that would passive-aggressively change her last name to win a fight with her current husband, it was my mother. I don't even think it counts as passive-aggressive, it's just plain aggressive.

"We were just about to eat," Ryan said, gesturing towards the dining table. He was trying to break the tension, but I wasn't sure inviting her in to eat with us was the best way to do it.

"What are you arguing about?" I asked. Ryan pulled out a chair for my mom and she lowered herself onto it, removing her large hat and placing it down on the ground next to the table legs. I wasn't sure how much my mom knew about my magical life now, she knew her sister had died and I think she had known she was a witch. It's been so long since we talked properly that I can't even remember what we last discussed.

"You can use your magic, darling," she smiled. Case closed. I clicked my fingers and another place setting appeared in front of my mother, the chili and rice pots hovered above the stove, floated over to the table and settled on two heat-proof mats. Ryan began to serve but I maintained a stony stare at my mom who still hadn't answered my question.

"Hello?" I prompted.

"This really is delicious," she said, taking a bite. "Edith pointed you in the direction of my favorite recipe I see, she must have warned you I was coming."

"No, she didn't," I snapped.

"Look, sometimes in a relationship it is hard for two adults with their own hopes and dreams to see eye-to-eye. Your stepfather and I are just going through a new phase in our lives and we are trying to find out what works best for both of us. Not all married couples run at the first sign of trouble," she snarked.

My blood was boiling. My mom and I generally got on well, but on the occasions when she was pushing all of my buttons at once, I could see why we had drifted apart. She was poking the bear on this particular topic, however.

"Greg and I didn't split over the first argument we ever had. You know that. We split up because he was cheating on me and had decided to start a family with his other woman, it wasn't a disagreement so much as a slap to the face," I snarled. "I would also like to remind you that you and dad got a divorce."

"Don't raise your voice, Nora. Come on now," she smiled, tilting her head to the side as if she was trying to convey sympathy and disappointment at the same time. Ryan's cell phone began to ring just as he cleared his plate, he apologized profusely.

"It's about 'Nutraspin', I have to take it," he said, shuffling out of the room and switching on his more professional work voice.

"Your husband seems nice, I thought I might have qualified for an invite to the wedding but I see you are quite different now, someone that doesn't need her mother, or manners!" she sneered.

"Mom, snap out of it. I know you go through these annoying phases of acting like a total snob any time you and Lee have been fighting, but I need you to knock it off. If you don't start acting like a nice person then you can get back on your scooter and buzz off back home," I huffed. "Ryan is not my husband either."

My mom rubbed at her eyes and her breathing suggested that she was fighting back tears. "I'm sorry, it was just... it's been our biggest fight so far. We usually fight over really trivial stuff, it's petty and pointless but we always get back together and love each other harder than before," she sniffed. "It doesn't feel like that this time."

"I'm sure things aren't as bad as they seem," I said, hoping to sound reassuring. Wiping away her own tears, she reached across the table and grabbed my hand.

"It sounds like you have your own problems."

"Huh?"

"Nutraspin? Your boyfriend works with Nutraspin, I would get out of there while you still can," she warned. Ryan came back in looking flustered. Mom let go of my hand and leaned back in her chair.

"I'm so sorry, I have to get into the office to clear up some paper-work. I think the other side is trying to bury us so they need all eyes on it before the court date this week," he sighed. He gave me a quick kiss on the cheek and waved goodbye to my mom as he made his way to the living room to gather up his things. "Thanks for dinner!" he shouted. Then we were alone.

"You really believe he is 'going to the office'," mom grunted. Her air quotes were dramatic and she looked like she had just started putting the final pieces of some puzzle together.

"Of course he is, what are you talking about?" I replied.

"You're first mistake was trusting someone, Nora. It's hardly your fault, that man is very attractive and I'm sure he had you under his spell within seconds of meeting you, not an *actual* spell of course, or maybe..."

"Mom, I trust Ryan. Whatever is going on with Lee has nothing to do with us. What happened between you two?" I asked. She looked down at her hands. It was the first time I realized that she wasn't wearing her wedding ring. She pressed the index finger and thumb of her right hand around the ring finger on her left, she was acknowledging the absence of that jewelry.

"I need to sleep, I was hoping I could stay here," she said.

"Of course you can," I smiled. Maybe their fight had been worse than usual this time. I said I would go and check on the guest room and invited her to raid the refrigerator for any dessert or late-night snacks that caught her eye. The house had a magical way of stocking up on the things it knew you needed. I heard squeals of delight as my mom discovered a tray of freshly baked snickerdoodles on the kitchen counter. I hadn't baked them.

On the way up to the guest room I noticed that Edith was appearing in every mirror along the corridor. In order to guarantee that she could visit me anywhere she liked, she had filled her home with mirrors before her death. She had suspected that someone was coming after her, and when she died her spirit was trapped in the mirrors of number thirteen Charm Close.

She had hidden the mirrors in closets, the attic and a few underneath the sofa. I had now hung up as many as I had space for, which gave me the impression that she was chasing me as I made my way to the guest room. I closed the door behind me so that we could speak in private, if she wanted anyone else to hear our conversation then she would have started speaking downstairs.

"What's up?" I asked.

"She doesn't look good," Edith said. My mom and Edith were sisters, I didn't know when they would have last spoke. Edith can only talk through the mirrors in this house and my mom hasn't visited me since I moved to Sucré.

"Some argument with Lee, it'll blow over I'm sure," I said. I pulled a fresh set of bedding from the linen closet and began to take the sheets off the mattress. I was aware that I could use my magic to do it all, but the physical process was a way to delay my return to the kitchen to face more mood swings from my mom.

My cell phone began to buzz in my pocket and I assumed it was Ryan. It wouldn't be a total surprise if he called me to say that he had faked a work emergency to get out of the awkward situation at the dinner table. It was a number I recognized, but not Ryan's.

"Dad?" I said, confused by the parent reunion I seemed to be having today.

"Nora, have you heard from your mother?" he asked. I could sense the concern in his voice. It wasn't as though their divorce had caused them to stop caring about each other, but in all the years since they split this had to have been the first time my dad had called me like this.

"Yeah, she just showed up like an hour ago," I said.

"How does she seem?" he pushed.

"Stressed out, upset and she's said some mean stuff, but I'm not taking it personally. She said her and Lee had a fight," I explained.

"About money? Don't give them any money!"

"What?"

"Nora, my secretary said that Lee called up asking to speak to me. When she asked him what it was regarding, he said that your mother had gotten into all sorts of debt and that she was about to sink them both. He was trying to get me to hand over tens of thousands of dollars. I said I would need to speak to her first but then he hung up."

I let the words sit with me for a moment. Debt? Had they been fighting about money? Why would they need so much cash to pay off what she owed, how could she have spent so much? It's not like I have that much money lying around, but why didn't she come to me for help? Is that why she was here now?

I felt awful for her, I'd seen all those documentaries about credit card debt and how difficult it can be to get out of that cycle. I also knew that my mom was too proud to come asking her daughter for that type of help. *Urgh.* How could I bring it up without saying that her ex-husband just called to snitch?

"She is going to stay with me for as long as she needs, if she brings up the money stuff then I'll deal with it then, but I don't know what I can do about it before then," I sighed. This was so unlike her, my mom had always been careful with her money, well, not *always* but she had gotten so much better. What could she have done that would have cost her so much?

"If your mother is involved with loan sharks then someone could come after her, if she has skipped town and is hiding out at your place then she is putting you at risk," he cried. Dad didn't know that I was a witch. I'm not claiming that I am above fear, obviously there is plenty of stuff that still scares me. I mean, my aunt was a witch and she still got murdered, but I don't worry about the same things that I used to.

"I'll call you back later," I whispered, hearing a noise by the door and worrying that my mom had overheard the entire conversation. It was Quin. He had a giant smile on his face and it seemed as though he had been eavesdropping.

"She's involved with the mafia, isn't she? She owes money, she has run away from where she lives *and* the garbage trucks came round today. Don't tell me that's just a coincidence!" he squealed.

Oh boy.

3

I was supposed to be going into the lab at the University where I worked today. I had been tasked with supervising students on a mock exam and I could honestly think of nothing worse. I made a few hurried phone calls as soon as I got out of bed, threw in the odd white lie about my mother being ill and then it was sorted, I had cover to take the day off.

I was hoping I hadn't brought bad luck our way, if my mom actually got sick now I would feel awful. I had a quick shower, wrapped a towel round my head and wandered down to the kitchen in my robe. My mom was already fully dressed with a full face of makeup and elegantly braided hair.

"What time did you get up?" I asked. A coffee machine that hadn't been there yesterday seemed to burst to life and the grinding sound meant that I couldn't hear her answer. We laughed as the seemingly never-ending sound continued. I walked over to collect my drink then joined her at the kitchen table.

"I got up early and went for a run," she smiled. "Then I got back, showered and got ready for the day. I just want to keep myself busy."

"Okay, well I have the day off so I can take you out to breakfast and show you around. I know that Edith probably gave you a tour at some point, but things might have changed," I said. I was already dreaming of heading to the bakery on the high street where Molly would whip us up a hot plate of something heavenly and all my troubles would melt away.

I didn't want to take my mother to Quin's café and have him bombard her with his mafia fantasies. I checked my watch, it was still too early for Molly's bakery to be open. I needed to kill some time and make sure both my mom and Quin didn't get into a fight about her mounting financial troubles.

"Would you be able to help me with a project? Part of my witch education involves some dumb bonding thing with Quin and they've suggested making a memory wall as part of it. I could use some help to work through photographs," I suggested.

"It still amazes me that this is your life now. I was always jealous of Edith, I wished that I could have abilities like she did. Her life seemed so full and interesting," she said, looking down at her own coffee and remembering her dead sister.

"You did all that travelling with Lee, your life was the one the rest of us were jealous of," I replied, wondering if mentioning the name of my stepdad would set her off again.

"That's the thing about comparisons, Nora. There is no way to win, there are no losers. You are chasing someone else's dream if you try to match every life experience, you can only do what makes you happy and celebrate the lives of those around you. Now you have Edith's magic, but is it giving you everything you wanted?" she asked.

I paused for a minute. "When I was going through my divorce, I didn't have hope. Nothing to look forward to. No direction. Now I feel like all of those worries are behind me and I am fulfilled in a way I wasn't before, it's not just because of magic though. Sometimes you have to do things outside of your comfort zone to move forward."

I wanted her to know that if she and Lee broke up, it wasn't the end of the world. It might feel like it for weeks, months even, but she would be okay.

"This boyfriend of yours is trapped in a pyramid scheme, Nora.

Nutraspin will ruin you just like it does with everyone else that gets caught up in it," she said sternly.

"Mom, he isn't working for them, he's a lawyer and there is a case being brought *against* them. He said one of the tactics can be to send over so much information, so many documents, that it is physically impossible to work through them all, that's why he got called back to the office last night," I said. I saw the fear vanish from her eyes, but it was replaced by a different feeling, one that I couldn't figure out.

"Oh well... that's great," she said, sitting up straighter and gazing briefly out of the kitchen window to the street. "Let's go dig through some pictures!" she declared, standing up and walking towards the stairs. She seemed to know where she was going so I followed her lead.

I pulled the towel off my head and my hair was now completely dry and styled in loose waves thanks to a shampoo spell that Ryan had taught me. I hadn't used my hairdryer in weeks, I'd taken one over to Ryan's house as more of a symbolic gesture.

My mom was heading straight for the attic. I made a quick detour to swap my robe for a long skirt and a t-shirt, then hurried to catch up. The attic space was a home library, filled with books on magic, cookbooks, some crime fiction and a worryingly large collection of vampire romance novels. It was only worrying because it made me think that Edith might know something about vampires that I don't, like, are they real? I still hadn't asked her.

My mom walked to the far wall and slid a panel over. I had never noticed it before, it was like a camouflaged closet door and behind it was a large trunk that she was now dragging into the room. I sat down on one of the chairs in the center, Quin appearing at the attic hatch and walking over to see what had been making all the noise.

"Right, where should we start?" mom said. I watched as she opened the trunk and the extent of the photography collection was revealed, it was a lot more chaotic than I had been hoping, but thankfully my mom seemed to have a good memory and began picking up pictures and describing the day they had each been taken.

Quin flicked his tail and the wall to our left was instantly cleared of objects and instead covered in cork board. A small tray of push pins appeared so that we could begin to put the pictures up. I could feel my curiosity building as mom picked up more and more of the photos, the smile on her face growing as she immersed herself in the past.

"Am I in any of them?" Quin yelled, he had batted a few of the push pins out of the tray and was now patting them gently as if he were suspicious that they might be something else.

"Do you get used to having a talking cat? Edith told me about it all, but I just can't imagine it becoming normal," mom chuckled.

"I actually have seven of them, the others have found a new park that isn't too far from the cat café in town where they all work. There is, and I quote, an 'untapped source of small birds' there. I don't want to know what they are doing to those tiny creatures, so I didn't ask many questions," I replied.

"Seven cats, well you always were a sucker for pets," mom said.

"I am not a pet, I am a familiar! I don't just sit around eating cat treats and getting scratches behind my ear!" Quin protested. I said nothing, but that *was* how he spent most of his time. I reached over to grab a photo that my mom had put down on the floor without comment. It was of me as a child with both of my parents and Edith.

I vaguely remembered a few trips with us all together like that, Edith never used magic in front of me when I was younger so it wouldn't have stood out as anything other than a regular family vacation. I decided that this was one that I was putting up on the wall.

Was now an appropriate time to lock down the exact reasons why my parents split? Probably not. My interest in knowing was the same as it has always been, but out of fear of upsetting someone I had never asked the question.

It wasn't a good time to ask about money either, despite the fact that I was holding a photograph of my mom standing in front of an expensive car. Had this been hers? When was this taken? My mom had the genetic gift of not aging at the same speed as other people, her face hadn't shown the effects of time over the last decade.

Wait, was that it? Had she paid for cosmetic surgery? I never would have been suspecting any of these things were it not for my dad's call.

"I thought there might be photos of my last trip to Mexico here," mom mumbled as she rifled through the trunk. All of the travelling that she and Lee had done together must have added up to a huge amount of cash, I had never questioned it before but how exactly could they afford it? My mom was retired as far as I knew, Lee had been in stable jobs all his life and mom said he had gone into consulting. Great pay less hours.

Quin was adding any picture of himself onto the cork board, he wasn't giving any explanation behind them. "Have you ever been on vacation, Quin?" I asked.

"Back when I was human, I quite liked those packages where someone collects you from the airport and takes you to a resort. I would sleep on the padded beds by the side of the pool and someone would bring me snacks. I think I went to Europe once, but I never left the resorts, so they all looked the same to me," he explained.

It was exactly what I would expect someone who *chose* to be a cat would say. Quin had been a human teacher before volunteering to become a familiar. It seemed that his interests and skills were better aligned with life as a talking feline, and the thought of him any other way didn't make any sense to me.

"Do you have pictures from when you were human?" I asked. Quin almost froze as if I had taken him completely by surprise. It seemed that he didn't want to talk too much about his human life and I got the impression that I had crossed a line. I felt as though getting him to open up about it would be an important part of the O.W.L. assignment.

My cell phone started to buzz again, this time it was Stacey from The Catmosphere Café.

"Hey Stacey, is everything okay?" I asked. She was a student at the University of Awa where I worked, she had taken on a part-time job at the café as we needed human bodies to serve the food so as not freak out the locals. Most regular people had never come across a talking cat before, let alone one that was making fruit pies.

"Yeah, there is a guy here looking for you. His name is Lee Jackson," she said. My stepdad was in town, no doubt he was hoping that I would show up to help run interference in this argument he was having with my mom. I could hear Stacey's footsteps as she walked away from wherever she had been standing, then I heard the office door close. She needed to speak to me privately.

"Nora, he is sweating and looks really nervous. Should I call the police? Or an ambulance?" Stacey said in hushed tones.

"It's my stepdad, he's probably fine. I'll be right over." I hung up and checked my watch. All of the businesses on the high-street would be coming to life by now so I could take my mom to Molly's café and then run over to see what was going on with Lee. If I'd known what was about to happen, I would have moved faster.

4

"*N*ora! I was hoping you would come in today, I have been meaning to talk to you about a business idea!" Molly announced as I walked into the café.

"I'm tied up with a million things at the moment, but I'd be happy to hear about it later. Sorry," I said, darting my eyes in my mother's direction hoping that it was clear what exactly was distracting me. Molly mouthed a silent *ah* and I brought my mom closer to the counter to select something to eat.

"Do you have any blueberry muffins?" my mom asked. Molly smiled her wide smile and retrieved one from the display. I nodded that I would take one as well, paid, and carried the muffins over to the table. I felt anxious about trying to sneak out of the café without making it obvious why I needed to leave, but I figured that it would be better for me to try and make sure everyone was level-headed before speaking to each other.

"One of the waitresses called me earlier, they said there is an issue with the safe. I'll just be a few minutes," I said. That seemed believable. I began to walk out of the door of the café and into the sunlight when someone grabbed my arm. I turned and realized that it was the other woman that worked with Molly.

"Did she try to talk to you about a business idea?" she asked.

"Molly? Yes, why?" I answered, flustered by the sudden conversation.

"Just don't get involved, if you have your head screwed on then keep out of it," she warned. She turned and walked back into the cafe. I heard her telling Molly that I had left my card at the counter and that she was returning it to me. Why had she lied? What had Molly been about to suggest?

I could worry about that later, I needed to fix my mom's marriage. Even as I thought it I realized it sounded stupid. It wasn't my job to force them to kiss and make up, if my mom really had tanked them financially then I doubted any amount of couples counselling would help him regain his trust in her.

I picked up the speed of my feet and jogged over to *The Catmosphere Café* only to be immediately mobbed by the other six familiars that lived with me. Voices shouted over each other as they ran around my ankles purring. I could barely make out a word any of them were saying. I had to assume that, as they were talking, there were no humans in the room.

"Nora, there you are," Stacey said. She looked like she had seen a ghost.

"Are you okay? Where is Lee?" I asked.

"He left," she whimpered. "I could sense something was going on, he was nervous and kept looking out of the window like he was expecting to see someone out there. I felt like his aura was dark, I could see a shadow over him that I haven't seen before. It scared me."

Stacey seemed to have some strange ability to read people, she could see the colors around them like a cloud, this usually was predictive of the future. If someone was clouded in darkness it would mean something terrible was about to happen. Whatever she had seen was new and terrifying.

"Sit down, I'll get you some water," I offered. Her hands trembled as she took the glass from me and I sat down beside her, giving her the space to process what had happened before sharing it with me.

"That man was troubled, I could feel it. He was giving off so much negativity that the air was tainted, something bad has happened to him already, before he even got here."

"I think he and my mom are fighting. They are both quite theatrical so even the smallest argument might make him react that way," I said.

"No, it was more than that," she protested.

"Did he say anything other than that he was looking for me? Anything about my mom?" I asked. Stacey shook her head. I really hoped this wasn't some elaborate prank by my dad, he hasn't always been the most supportive person when it came to my mom getting re-married. His opinion seemed to change with the wind depending on his own personal life. Maybe *he* was having a string of bad luck and projecting it onto them.

"He just said that he would be looking for a hotel if he couldn't get hold of you," she said. I thought about the only hotel nearby and didn't want to put him through it, but I could hardly force my mom to accept his presence in the house. It was my house though... "He wanted to buy your mom flowers, I remember him saying that. I pointed him in the direction of the florist."

"How long ago was that?" I asked.

"Maybe ten or fifteen minutes ago," she replied. That meant he was probably still there. I've been to that flower place; I wouldn't say speedy service was at the top of their priority list. I thanked Stacey, asked the cats to do something to keep her mind off the meeting with my stepdad and ran out onto the street again.

I was going to have to travel past Molly's café on the way there. This would make it harder to explain why I had left my mom to eat breakfast by herself as my lie would be exposed. My mom had been sitting in the window, but as I got closer to the café, even from across the road, I could see that she wasn't there anymore.

I slowed down and tried to get a better look but she didn't seem to be in there at all. I needed to get to Lee before I lost him, my mom was probably just chatting with Molly somewhere that was obstructed by the window frame or a vase of flowers. As I walked past the general store, Jane, one of the cashiers, hurried out to speak to me.

"Nora, your stepdad is looking for you," she yelled. I stopped walking and turned on my heels to face her.

"He's been in there too?" I asked, pointing at the store.

"Yeah, about ten minutes ago maybe, he was looking for Turkish delight," she answered. He had been shopping for my mom's favorite type of candy, he was in the store looking for more gifts to try and win her over. If she was the one racking up all the debt, why was Lee trying to apologize?

"Thanks Jane," I sighed. "If you see him just give me a shout, I'm trying to track him down. I don't know why he doesn't just call my cell phone."

"I said the same thing to him, he muttered something about cell phones being *'the way they get you'*, then left the store. He seemed like a conspiracy theory nut, no offense," she smiled.

"None taken, don't worry. Him and my mom are both on another planet most of the time, but now they are forcing me to get involved in their bickering," I grumbled as I waved and walked away. Great, Lee was under the impression that cell phones were the enemy and I have a cat convinced that the garbage men of this town are caught up in money laundering. I should make the pair of them some foil hats.

When I arrived at the flower shop the owner was moving at a pace I hadn't seen before. Shuttling from one side of the shop to the other, building a wall of flower display items as if re-carving a path on the ground to re-direct foot traffic.

"Herb? What's happening?" I asked. The owner was a man in his sixties, his body seemed to have aged beyond his years and was usually causing him to travel slowly and speak even slower. Something had caused him to be rushing around the place and I had to assume he was on a new medication, or he was up to something.

"Nora, you shouldn't be here, you can't be here when they come," he flapped. "You don't want to get in the way of the authorities."

"What authorities?" I said.

"The police! I bet they bring others too, the FBI and maybe the coastguard! Well... the coastguard is not the right one, but you understand what I'm saying, right?"

"It's as clear as mud. Let me help, what's the problem? Why are the police coming?" I asked, assuming that there was some toxic gas in Sucré's air that was making everyone in town suspicious and paranoid.

"A man is dead Nora!" he shrieked. "Murdered!"

"What? Okay, let's not jump to conclusions. Where is this man?" I asked. I wanted to maintain the belief that this was all the ramblings of someone that was under the influence of mass hysteria, but I was getting a sense that something truly terrible had happened.

I was looking for my stepdad, he had been working his way to the flower shop over the last fifteen minutes and suddenly there is a dead man in here? I needed to believe that Herb was overreacting. He began to move some of the flower displays that he had just place in the center of the room. I saw a foot.

I didn't recognize the shoe, but why would I? It would have been more bizarre if I had memorized the footwear of everyone in town. I had been working as a private investigator in my spare time, breaking curses and locating missing keys. It had been quite tame so far, not what I had expected. This seemed more in line with what I was looking to work on.

Since I moved to Sucré I had stumbled upon dead bodies at every turn, then become entangled in the case until there was an arrest or an answer to the mystery. It had been dangerous and scary, but worth it for the sense of achievement that I would feel once justice was delivered.

Herb continued to move objects to reveal more of the man on the ground. He was wearing a dark green waterproof coat, a wedding ring on his finger a few inches below an expensive watch. His face was obscured by a large pair of garden scissors protruding from his chest. *Gruesome.*

Despite having been involved in so many murder cases, I had never come across a crime scene where the murder weapon had been left for all to see. As horrible as this was, there was a chance that there were fingerprints on the handles of the scissors. They were so huge, better suited for trimming hedges than flowers for a bouquet, but it was sensible to assume they had been taken from the flower shop and used as an impromptu killing tool.

I stepped sideways and the face of the victim was revealed. It was Lee. I took a sharp breath inward and staggered back, supporting myself on the cash register as the blood left my head and I felt dizzy. Lee. My stepdad had been murdered. How could this be happening? He had been in town for less than an hour, did he know anyone around here expect me?

I felt the tears rolling down my cheeks as I flashed through the memories we had together, shaking at the thought of breaking the news to my mom. I could hear sirens now, that had to be an ambulance. There was a police station in the center of town, they could probably walk here now and still beat the EMTs.

My mother stepped through the entrance of the flower shop at the same time as my ex-boyfriend, Officer Brent Murphy. She screamed and Brent wrapped his arms around her to stop her running forward and compromising the crime scene. Herb was standing at my side.

"They were arguing," Herb said. I turned to look at him, wiped the tears from my eyes and waited for him to elaborate. "She came in, they were shouting. I went into the back to give them some privacy and I got caught up watering some plants back here. When I came back out onto the shop floor, he was dead." What was he implying?

Was my mom the killer?

5

I had my arms around my mom as we were asked to step outside. Brent kept making movements that suggested he wanted to come and speak to me. When his back up finally arrived, he hurried out to the sidewalk and stood beside us. I was holding it together better than I expected, but my mom was completely silent.

She wasn't crying, she didn't look sad or distressed. Just numb. Everyone reacts differently to these types of things, grief affects us all in unique ways. Her grief looked a lot like disinterest though.

"Nora, am I able to speak to you?" Brent asked. Another officer wandered out to stand with my mom. I stepped away and Brent followed, once there was a few feet of clearance around us it was clear that he felt able to speak. "That's your stepdad, isn't it?"

Of course he would remember, it's not as if the house was lined with photographs from my childhood, but I had shown him pictures of my parents. A lot of the pictures I have of my mom have Lee standing right beside her. I nodded.

"Herb has already given us a brief timeline, so I know that you walked in on him trying to block the body from view. It would still be good if you could come to the station for some more questions," he said. I could tell from the tone of his voice that he was trying to pepper in as much sympathy as possible, but I had to assume that Herb had also mention that my mom had been in the store yelling at Lee just before he was killed.

"I can do that, what about my mom? Do you need me to come in now?" I asked.

"One of my colleagues has had some additional training for dealing with bereaved individuals that are present at body discovery. It happens more often than you'd think," he explained.

Reading between the lines, I guessed that Brent wanted a special officer to speak to my mom because they think she killed him. Not just a straight-forward 'caught red handed' crime, but perhaps the money stuff that my dad had mentioned meant that this was all more complicated. But could the Sucré police know about their financial situation already?

I turned to see my mom being escorted down the street by Emma, Brent's fiancé who was also a police officer. It wasn't the time to focus on how awkward it was to be in the same space as my ex-boyfriend and his new love. Brent walked over to his patrol car and held open the back door.

"Sorry, I can't let you ride in the front. Department policy," he said, giving a gentle smile as he knew it looked as if I was being quietly arrested. I climbed into the back and wondered if I should call Ryan to request that he act as my legal representation. Was that even allowed? This was exactly the sort of thing Ryan would be able to answer if he were here.

"What will happen to my mom?" I asked. Brent looked at me via the rearview mirror and spoke while facing the road.

"We just need to ask some questions, establish if the vict—sorry, if your stepfather had any enemies, if anyone had reason to want him dead. Until we start looking into it, we only have access to the surface level facts and sometimes that is enough for us to solve a case," he explained.

"What does 'looking into it' look like?" I asked.

"I can't really discuss that with you, I'm sorry," he replied. I believed him, he really wanted to share more with me, but he was more focused on bringing the killer to justice. I was just concerned that the killer might be my own mother and I felt compelled to defend her. "We have an address for you stepdad that is, wow, this is hours away," he said, looking over quickly at his notepad on the passenger seat.

"Yeah, I speak to him and my mom on speakerphone calls every now and then but a lot of the time they are travelling so I wait to get the photos from their trip. I haven't been to their home in quite a while," I confessed. I felt guilty, as if my presence alone would have prevented the two of them arguing.

We pulled up outside the police station, walked inside and sloped off into a side room for a sit-down conversation. I wasn't sure if I was under suspicion now too.

"Are they both visiting for an occasion?" he asked. This felt like it wasn't relevant to the investigation, I mean, of course it was relevant, but it also felt like my ex-boyfriend was trying to figure out if I had gotten engaged in secret. I shook my head and he wrote something down. "Do you know of any financial troubles that he might have been in?"

I paused. I became hyper aware of my every move as I feared Brent might know more about all this than he was letting on. My dad seemed to think mom had driven them deep into debt and maybe this was a reason for her to lash out, maybe Lee had been giving her a hard time about it, or maybe he had a big life insurance policy that would cover all of the money my mom owed. If I lied to the police then I could be implicated in this whole thing.

As if he had heard my silent cry for help, Ryan came into the room and sat beside me. "I was wondering when you'd show up," Brent said, his tone abrasive.

"I would like to speak to my client," Ryan said. He wasn't acknowledging Brent's hostility and his proximity to me made me feel instantly calmer. I had just been about to lie to the police, maybe that's why Ryan showed up. His priority would be to protect me, he might not have the same motivation to keep my mom out of jail.

Brent closed his note pad, stood up and walked out of the room.

Ryan waited until he was gone before throwing himself around me and squeezing so tightly that I could barely speak.

"I'm so sorry. Are you okay? Is your mom okay? I should have been with you this morning but I've been so busy with my stupid job," he rambled. I struggled against his grip so that he would loosen it, then replied.

"I'm fine. I think the shock has kept me going, there will be a moment when I truly realize what happened today, what I saw…"

"I heard. I can only imagine what that must have felt like," he said, lowering his head and holding both my hands. I felt as though he was having a more emotional response than I was, but he was detached from it by a degree so could see the bigger picture. My mind was focused on the potential guilt of my mom; the time for tears would be after all this.

"Do you trust me?" I asked.

"Of course," he replied without hesitation.

"I have to do something that you may consider unethical, it probably goes against your lawyer code or whatever," I began. "But I need to know if you want to be involved or if it's better than you stay out of it."

"Will you be in danger if you do this thing?" he asked.

"Possibly, I really don't know."

"If you are at risk, then I'm there," he said. "Let me get you out of this police station and we can talk properly."

"What about my mom?" I asked.

"I've already gotten her out, I pushed her 'emotional distress' as a reason to question her later so she is waiting in my car outside. She is probably having some really low moments by herself so we should hurry up," he said. Ryan darted out of the room and I was barely alone for an entire minute before he returned with news that I could leave.

Brent was standing behind the reception desk as we walked out of the station and I could sense that he wasn't happy with the way that had all gone down. He had inherited powers from a relative not too long ago and I wondered if his abilities included knowing if people were lying or not. I felt as if I was sweating through my clothes, but soon I was outside and away from the eyes of the police.

My mom was sitting in the back seat of Ryan's car and I shuffled into the shotgun spot, turned and saw her face as pale as I had ever seen it. It was as if every drop of color had been drained from her body and even the shine of her eyes had dimmed. She might not be hysterically crying like they do in the movies, but she was clearly heartbroken.

Ryan began to drive us back to my house, it was only a short trip but it seemed as though walking back along the high street past the flower shop would have caused us all to freak out. Ryan made the journey longer by taking extra turns to avoid driving past the police tape.

I hoped that Quin wasn't at the house, he can occasionally be a source of comfort, but he also is generally oblivious to other people's feelings and he isn't famous for being able to read the room. Ryan pulled up outside the house on Charm Close and I jumped out to help my mom from her seat. It was as if her body was working but she wasn't living in there anymore. She was an empty shell.

Quin seemed to have gone out on one of his adventures. If I got a call from the town sanitation department that he was driving through their garbage trucks again I would be livid.

Ryan and I guided my mom up the steps, through the door and into the living room. She sat down on the sofa and we sat on chairs facing her so that we could talk. I didn't know what to say, or what to ask. My mom looked up at me and seemed to be filtering through her mind to find the words she wanted to get out.

"He was in debt," she uttered. "I don't know exactly how much, but it was almost six figures. It got worse and worse and he kept it all a secret from me, I only found out by accident by picking up a letter that was sent to the house with no name, just our address. He had put our house up as collateral, taken money from loan sharks, I don't even know how bad this is. I found out last week and now he is dead."

"*Lee* was in debt?" I asked.

"Yes," she confirmed.

"He called dad asking for money, he said that *you* were the one that had got them into a mess," I said. She scoffed in disbelief.

"Did he ask that your father not mention it to me?" she said, a look of disbelief spreading across her face. I nodded. "Nora, we were probably days away from having our home taken from us, all of our savings are gone. The fact that he was secretly calling your father is news to me, but not entirely surprising. It seems as though Lee was a master at lying."

My brain scanned through every true crime documentary I had ever seen and money was a huge motive for murder in most of them. If what she was saying was true, then this worked against her in the eyes of the police. If Lee had financially ruined them both then she was the number one suspect, even I was having doubts.

"Mom, this is crazy… I don't know what to say."

"Sweetheart, you don't even know the half of it," she sighed.

6

Ryan made us coffee and my mom went to wash her face. She said the cool water would help her feel more alive, or as alive as she could considering what had happened this morning. Ryan came back into the room and put the mugs down on the table in the center of the rug.

"What do you think she means? What do you think he did to get into so much debt?" Ryan whispered. I shrugged. I had spent every moment since the phone call with my dad thinking that my mom had been blowing all their money on vacations and Botox, but now I felt cripplingly guilty that I hadn't questioned dad's version of events.

As she came back she was able to muster a smile before sitting down again.

"Where should I start?" she asked.

"You said you found stuff out last week, right? Maybe just work through the timeline from that point, what happened, what you know, what you think has happened to Lee," Ryan answered. He was thinking rationally, I wasn't able to yet.

"It all started with a cup of coffee, funnily enough," she said, picking up her mug and taking a sip. "I was working on some emails at my computer when there was a noise outside, a loud dog or something, and I whipped my body around to look out of the window, only to knock the coffee right across the keyboard. We had talked about me getting a new computer anyway, so I wasn't heart-broken about it, but I had been in the middle of doing something important.

"So, with Lee out of the house, I figured I would just use his computer," she sighed. I felt like I knew where this was going. "I clicked on the email icon like I would on my own computer, only it was obviously not logged into my account, but Lee's."

She took another long sip of coffee.

"Is this going to incriminate you?" Ryan interrupted. She chuckled then shook her head.

"No, it's just embarrassing more than anything else. Although I suppose a police officer would see things differently. I found a number of emails from Nutraspin first of all. I thought he might have been trying to lose a bit of weight or something, I had heard the name of the company before but it didn't sound like something he would be into.

"It wasn't just a case of him buying a few packets of the milkshake mix, he was ordering hundreds of boxes. I kept looking through the emails and then started to make a note of the figures, adding them up to try and see what was happening. Then I found an email from a storage unit company asking if he wanted to extend his lease."

I was now leaning back in my chair trying to keep hold of the details. This all seemed so strange and I couldn't put the clues together yet, but Ryan seemed to know.

"Did he have platinum status?" Ryan asked.

"He did," mom smiled. "I guess this is common then, I hadn't heard of it before."

"What are you talking about?" I said, sitting forward.

"Nutraspin..." Ryan said, "is essentially a pyramid scheme. Someone will have recruited Lee and promised him all these benefits, extra money and freedom to choose your own hours. The selling point when recruiting is telling people that the harder they work, the more they can make. If you have been working a salaried job your entire life then this sounds appealing, I bet Lee had worked overtime for free in the past, right?"

"Yes, plenty of times. He worked weekends too, on short notice, with no extra pay. Then all of a sudden the overtime stopped and I should have questioned it, but he said he had been promoted and that I didn't need to worry about him being home late for dinner again," she explained. "I should have pushed it further, but I didn't."

"Pyramid schemes make their money through recruiting, not through actually selling much product," Ryan continued. "You make more cash if you can convince people to work under you, then if they make any sales you get a cut, as does the person above you and the person above them. If you don't know that going in, then you can get caught up in the lies and convince yourself that you are doing something good for your family, it's brutal to watch. I've been reading through this company's history and it's heartbreaking."

"I have to assume that he had targets with recruiting or sales and he wasn't meeting either, so he decided to pretend that he was making sales. He bought the stuff with his own cash then hid it with the intention of selling it later on. Platinum status got you free tickets to the conventions all over the US," he said.

"That's why we went on so many vacations. He would only need to cover the flights and hotel, but got a free ticket to the event, so I would hang out by the pool while he 'took care of some business.' I just..." she tailed off.

"Having platinum status is sold as this elite level that gives you access to all these benefits that the lower levels don't get. So if Lee was seen to be making over a certain level of sales, he would have been given access to the convention, probably a car allowance and maybe his cell phone bill was covered by the company," Ryan said. Mom nodded in agreement.

"Why would he do that? I don't understand. So he bought a ton of milkshake powder, spent all that money, for someone to cover his phone bill?" I said, struggling to wrap my head around it.

"You are looking at it as an outsider. Once those people get their hooks into you, they can convince you of anything. They are experts at ego massage. Imagine your job treats you like garbage for years and then someone comes along with an offer to remove all of those inconveniences, all those stressors, but allow you to earn more money and spend more time with your family. You would jump at the chance. You also wouldn't want to disappoint them, so you might do something unwise," Ryan huffed.

I could see why Ryan had been having such a tough time recently. If his case at work had involved hours of reading through testimony of people that had been screwed over by Nutraspin then I was surprised he hadn't come home crying. They had taken advantage of Lee and now he was dead.

"That's not all," mom huffed. "I don't think I even know everything yet, but his laptop will be back at the house and the police will be all over it soon. I think he was having an affair."

"What?" I shrieked.

"He was corresponding with a woman, someone called 'C', I only got the chance to read one of their messages before he came back and caught me at his computer. I confronted him about the shakes, asked him where he was getting the money for all these purchases and then he went silent. I pulled out my cell phone and checked the balance on our credit cards, they were all maxed out. I asked him to tell me how deep this went and that's when he told me the pensions were gone."

"What do we do now? If there is evidence on the computer that Lee was cheating on you then it is going to be really hard to convince the police that you didn't kill him. The motive here would be hard to ignore," I moaned.

"We should look at the laptop, see if we can get in there and sort out the money situation. I can take you on as a client and then it is part of my job to defend you. You are a victim of this company as much as Lee was," Ryan announced. I felt my heart pound in my chest. The worry I'd had that he wouldn't fight as hard to defend her was wrong, I felt stupid for even thinking it.

"Is that legal?" she asked.

"Leave that to me. We should get in the car and head over to the house now, seize the laptop and then claim that it was a shared device.

That way it's reasonable that you would have access to it and want to utilize it. We can sort through the emails, try to see how deep this goes with Nutraspin, add it to my class suit and then try to get you out of this debt," he smiled.

Whether this was a dumb idea or not, I was into it. If there was even a chance that Ryan could get my mom out of financial ruin then I had to help him. Quin wandered back into the house as we stood up to leave.

"Well, well, well, I see that you are all having a cozy hang out without me. I guess it's truly out of sight out of mind with you guys, huh? Don't mind me, I'll just wander up and down the high street looking for company and then almost get hit by a speeding police car. It must have been going almost ten miles per hour, it could have killed me!" Quin yelled.

"Quin!" I shouted back. I beckoned him over to the kitchen while my mom put on her coat and shoes. "Look, my stepdad was murdered a few hours ago, that's why there are police everywhere."

"What did you do this time?" he scowled.

"Why on earth would you think I had anything to do with it?!" I snapped. "Look, we are about to go to my mom's house, do you want in or not?"

"Obviously I want to come with you, what am I going to do around here on my own? Well, I only have five episodes left of this hospital drama I've been watching online. I decided to watch them out of order, so like season four episode two, then the pilot episode, then the third episode of season six. I have absolutely no idea what's going on, sometimes everyone is friends with a character, then they all hate him, and I don't know why," he laughed.

"I don't even... just get in the car," I huffed. Ryan was waiting in the driver's seat, we all piled in and mom gave him the address. He typed it into his navigation system and then we hit the road. Quin and my mom seemed to be locked in an endless conversation about Edith and I was beginning to think the two of them would be better suited for my bonding assignment than I was.

At some point it became clear that everyone was hungry, my mom was using the conversation with Quin to distract herself from what had happened this morning and I worried that there would be a point when it all hit her and she would break down.

"Cibus," I said, holding out my hands in anticipation of the incoming meal. Three full sized burritos landed on my palms, and a smaller one for Quin. My mom was grinning from ear to ear, presumably because she hadn't seen me perform much magic yet and was fascinated by the whole thing.

We were soon pulling up to my mom's house and I looked over to see her lowering her food, this was going to be emotionally grueling, but necessary. Ryan stopped the car and I saw a tear fall down her face, it was becoming real now. Once she showed us what was on that computer, she had to accept that everything had really happened, there wouldn't be a way to pretend it wasn't real.

We just had to hope that we could get in and out before the police got here. That shouldn't be too hard, right?

7

We hurried inside and closed the door behind us. Ryan had parked his car in the garage to keep it off the street and away from prying eyes, but we had probably been noticed already. Quin was in his element, rubbing his body up against any object in the house, which was not ideal considering he was leaving fur all over everything. The plan was to pretend we were never here.

My mom was standing on the welcome mat that was pushed up against the front door. They had one both inside and outside just to make sure no mud got onto their carpeting. She seemed unwilling to move further into the house, no doubt there were photographs of her and Lee plastered across the walls and it would be painful to see them. Her last memory of him was the state his body was in at the flower shop.

"Where is the laptop?" Ryan asked. That seemed to snap her out of the zombie trance. She kicked her shoes off and began to walk through the living room. This wasn't my childhood home, this was a place they had bought together sometime during my college years. I had a room here, but it wasn't filled with boy band posters and jewelry boxes with spinning ballerinas.

The living room was tastefully decorated, by that I meant plain.

The walls were a soft, off-white with beige picture frames wrapped around paintings of landmarks they had visited. A colorful picture of the Eiffel Tower in the rain was my favorite. The wedding pictures were scattered across shelves or on tables. It seemed like a show home, like it hadn't been lived in by messy, normal people.

The living room branched off towards the kitchen and an office space to the right. Mom tried the door, but it wouldn't budge.

"It's locked, we never lock this door. Why would he lock it?" she said.

"He had something to hide, don't worry about this," I said. I wrapped my fingers around the handle. "Regino!" The handle loosened and I turned it, hearing the mechanism inside moving. I pushed my way into the room.

Considering how neat and tidy the rest of the house was, this place was wild. It was as if every slob impulse they both had had been suppressed everywhere else, but in here it was a free for all. The desk was littered with scraps of paper, piles of documents teetered on the windowsill and on the ground around the legs of the office chair and coffee rings stained the wood beside the laptop.

It was at least a relief to know that even the tidiest of people had to let loose every once in a while. Ryan didn't seem to see things that way. "Was the room like this before you left?" he asked.

"No, we have a system for our… I don't even know where half of this stuff has come from," she gasped.

Ryan's sharp eyes dissected the room. "He was panicking, something must have changed, and he needed to look through all of these papers in a hurry. He looked through all this, then rushed over to Sucré to find you," Ryan explained. "That means that somewhere in this pile of stuff is a potential clue."

"…Do you have any hints as to where a clue would be?" I asked, staring at the mountains of papers in front of us. Even if we were to skim read all of it, it would take hours between us. Ryan sat in the chair and thought for a moment.

"One of us needs to go through the laptop, I think that should be me. Can you both get started on the documents down here? I don't know how long it will be before we get company in the form of the police department, so we need to move quickly. Quin, can you keep a look out?" Ryan asked. That was overly optimistic in my opinion, trusting a job so important to Quin when he was still rubbing his face against door frames and purring.

Quin nodded and trotted off, but who knows where he was actually going. I didn't feel like risking being arrested because my familiar couldn't focus, but we couldn't waste time by having one of us sit by the front window. Ryan pulled the chair close to the laptop, opened it, and began using his magic to bypass the password entry screen.

I think the determination to find clues that might lead to an explanation as to why Lee was killed was enough to get my mom moving. She sat cross-legged on the floor and picked up a handful of paper to start looking through.

I sat beside her and grabbed a few to read, not sure if I would understand that I would recognize a clue if I saw one.

I had been working as a private investigator as a side gig, but that didn't usually involve diving into a case with no preparation. Lee had been murdered hours ago and now we were rifling through his stuff to look for answers, it probably wasn't going to be all that simple and I had to stay positive for everyone else's sake.

I picked up a handwritten order form for one box of Nutraspin. Then another. Then an order for three boxes. They all had different handwriting, or at least at first glance it looked that way. I looked over at my mom and she seemed to be realizing the same thing that I was. Lee had faked some orders by changing up his own handwriting to pretend he was different people.

"How many have you got so far?" I asked mom.

"I think this adds up to about twenty boxes of the stuff, but he has written all of these," she replied.

"I have emails here where he has attached copies of the order forms to HQ. It seems that for some of the smaller orders it is expected that the customer fills out the paperwork and Lee would send it in order to complete the sale under his reference code," Ryan said. "For the larger ones he probably didn't need to bother messing about with different colored pens."

"Do you have records of the larger sales?" I asked.

"I'm still skimming through correspondence with his line manager. She is singing his praises for this one here, look. He sent over an order for over two hundred boxes that were being bought by a local gym. He has another one for sixty boxes for a wellness spa in town," Ryan said. "This is a trail we will need to follow, we need to see if *any* of these larger orders are real. We need to get into his storage unit too."

"Have you got the address for that?"

"Not yet, still rifling through his spam mail. He didn't separate his inboxes, I don't even know how you do that. Most of this stuff is junk but it's all going into the same area as his regular mail," he complained.

"He liked signing up for newsletters, anything that was related to business magazines or self-help websites. He would drive me crazy telling me about some new startup company he had seen interviewed online, I didn't realize how badly he wanted to be his own boss. I just thought he was aiming higher within the company he worked for," mom said.

"Yeah, about that…" Ryan sighed, turning the chair to face us. "It looks like he lost his job last year. I think there was an overlap of about three months where he signed up to be a Nutraspin representative and then getting fired. From these emails here it seems that his work performance took a nosedive, probably because he was too busy trying to sell milkshakes."

"He lost his job?" mom gasped. "Why wouldn't he tell me? It would be funny if it wasn't so sad, he was dealing with so much by himself."

"It looks like he has been living on credit cards for years mom," I said. "Look." I passed over a pile of card statements that showed the amount of credit each company had given him, and his attempts to make the minimum payments had just about kept their heads above water. He had probably been a few thousand dollars in the red for a long time, but then it got worse as he maxed them out to buy product from a pyramid scheme.

Mom took the pages one at a time and looked at the payments. "He paid for wedding anniversary gifts with this, birthday dinners, this is the hotel we stayed at after he pretended he had gotten a promotion at work. This… this is that holiday to Hawaii that he took me on for valentine's day last year."

"I've got the address of his storage unit. Look, we need to take the computer for sure, but I don't know about all these papers," Ryan said.

"We should leave a few bank statements, make it clear that it was his debt," I suggested.

"That only puts the nail in my coffin. If the police can easily see what a mess he made then it will be easier for them to blame me," mom protested.

"Guys, I hate to interrupt, you know me," Quin interrupted. "But two huge police vans pulled up outside a few minutes ago and I think they are planning to surround the place. They were talking for a while but I got distracted by a house fly."

"What? Are you kidding?" I yelled.

"I don't kid," he scoffed, as if *I* were being ridiculous.

"How do we get out? We can't just get in the car and drive away. We can't just make a break for it either because the car is in the garage and they would know we were here!" mom shouted. She was panicking now and understandably so. Whatever trouble Ryan and I might get into for hiding a potential murderer would be nothing compared to my mother tampering with evidence in a case for which she is the main suspect.

"Mom, did you forget who you are with?" I smirked. "I'll get us out, can you take care of the car?" I asked Ryan. He nodded and closed his eyes to focus on the task. "Mom, hold this, I'll grab some papers. This is all we have to go on, so hold tight. If we leave something important behind then we might not get another chance to come back."

When Ryan re-opened his eyes I thrust a pile of paper at him and then picked Quin up under one arm, leaning towards Ryan so that my elbow could make contact with him, and reaching out my left leg to hook it around my mom's calf. With the three of us all connected, I focused on number thirteen Charm Close and closed my eyes.

I felt the air rushing past my face. The sound of knocking growing louder and louder. The police were about to come in and we would get arrested on the spot, I had no doubt. When the movement stopped and I opened my eyes, the knocking continued. There was a police officer knocking on the front door of my house, I recognized the hat in the silhouette through the glass.

"Ryan," I whispered. He took the papers and laptop in a giant mound in his arms and began to run up the stairs towards the attic. The attic would seal itself off from humans if it needed to, so anything we had stolen from the house would remain undetected.

I smoothed down my clothes, tucked a few stray hairs behind my ears and answered the door. Standing there were two officers, one of which was Brent's fiancé Emma.

"Ms. Jackson, we are placing you under arrest for the suspected murder of Lee Jackson. Anything you…" Emma began. I froze, my mind strangely quiet as I tried to think of something to say or do. This couldn't be happening.

8

I had tried to protest. Of course I had. Ryan had held me back and pointed out that we would both be of more use if we didn't get arrested, so I stopped the shouting and screaming and promised to get her out as quickly as I could. It was a promise I hoped I could keep.

I sat on the bottom step of the stairs and tried to steady my breathing, I was so sure she hadn't hurt Lee, but there was this unshakeable speck of doubt that I couldn't ignore. Herb had seen her in that flower shop just moments before he was killed, I needed to build a timeline in her defense. It would be tight, only a margin of error of a few seconds, not even minutes.

"Nora, we need to go to this storage unit," Ryan said. I blinked away the images of my mother in handcuffs and looked up at him.

"Why?"

"We need to figure out exactly who Lee was involved with. He maxed out the credit cards, he had taken all their savings to try and pay off debts and continue buying those stupid shakes, but he was still making some payments on bills and affording to take them on those conference trips. This job with Nutraspin wasn't bringing in any money; we need to find out where he was getting cash," he explained.

I sighed and stood up. The only thing that would help my mom was going to be the two of us taking action.

"Fine, I'll come," Quin huffed. "But I think you should know that sometimes those storage units are full of mice, so I will be busy chasing those, I won't be looking through paperwork. That sounds super boring. Is your mom a murderer now? That's nuts. I mean, I always figured if anyone was taking bets on which member of the family would be getting arrested for murder, I'd be putting my money on you, again. How many times have you been arrested now?" he asked me.

"Once!" I replied. "Just the once. You might remember that I didn't kill that woman, I just was the number one suspect for a while. Just like that, my mom is innocent too."

"Yeah, your voice doesn't sound all that sure," Quin laughed.

"You are the most annoying creature on the planet," I huffed. I had to hand it to him though, he had distracted me enough that I was feeling able to focus on the next task instead of dwelling on the whole 'mom in jail' situation.

"Right, the storage unit is back by your moms place, I don't think we should be seen to be driving over that way again. The police will be all over it soon and they will be checking cameras for car plates. You will need to transport us again," Ryan said. "I've got the address, you just need to take us to an area near to it, and then we can walk over. Maybe somewhere out of sight, like a wooded area or something."

"Want me to juggle while I'm at it?" I teased. He smiled, he was putting a lot of faith in me to be able to pull off that spell twice and I wasn't sure I had the strength to do it. There would only be one way to find out. I picked up Quin who immediately began wriggling in my arms as if it was a surprise that I had lifted him off the ground. I tucked him under my left arm like a football and grabbed onto Ryan's hand, weaving my fingers between his.

"We need to head to 'Squirrel Storage', or a spot close to it. It's unit 42," Ryan said. I nodded and closed my eyes. It was all on me to get us there. I couldn't have my mom in prison, the faster I proved that it wasn't her, the better.

I felt an ache across my body like the muscle fatigue after a workout, it felt more of an effort to summon the powers that would transport us to a town hours away. I had only just done it, there had barely been a forty-minute rest. The further I was required to travel, the harder it was. It was as though I had used up my quota of magic for the day.

I strained to make it happen, but the familiar rush of cold air over the skin on my face brought me instant relief. When I felt my feet thud onto the ground I laughed slightly, it wasn't quite the soft landing we were used to. I opened my eyes and the laughter stopped. Where were we?

"Err, Nora?" Quin began. "Do you have any clue as to where you have dumped us? This seems like it is *not* near a storage unit. Some would argue that this is a field full of sunflowers in fact."

"I see that," I hummed, looking left and right and seeing only green stalks reaching up towards the sky and a sea of yellow petals above us. This was true in every direction. I looked over at Ryan who was bouncing up and down as if on an invisible pogo stick, desperately trying to find a direction for us to follow. "Well?"

"We are right in the middle of this field, no doubt about it," he smiled. "In your defense, I did say we should arrive in a place where no one would see us. This is pretty much exactly what I asked for."

"And…that is why I did this," I laughed. "I'm just so tired, I mustn't have had enough energy to get us any closer. Are we even in the right town?"

"I can smell the house we were in earlier, we aren't too far away," Quin added. Thank goodness we brought him. It was a thought I rarely had, but he was actually being useful. "I can guide us back to the house, or at least the street if we need to stay back because the cops are there."

"That would be great, I thin—"

"Or maybe we are in Alaska, or Amsterdam?" Quin interrupted. *Oh boy.* "Did you know that I can speak Dutch? I have literally so many skills it would sizzle your mind."

"I don't need you to describe a windmill to me right now, I need you to take us to a place we recognize. Please?" I asked. Quin shrugged and began walking through the stalks, Ryan and I followed, weaving one way then another to fit in the spaces that Quin was strolling into. We could hear voices in the distance, excited voices of young people. Were we near a school?

The sunflowers seemed just as thick right up until we were walking across the dirt at the edge of the field. The voices had been from a bunch of teenagers that were barking orders at their cell phone-wielding friends for different angles of their pouting faces for a sunflower photo shoot.

I wanted to yell something about how these photo-opportunities were probably the reason why the flowers by this fence looked so limp and damaged, but I resisted. The less attention I brought to us the better. They didn't even notice us emerge from the field, scale the fence and loudly land on the other side. Quin had made it look effortless, of course. He had the 'four legs and a tail' advantage, so I wasn't expecting that I would be as graceful a climber as he was.

I recognized the houses, we were close to my mom's neighborhood. When I had moved back into the house for my college summers, I had been so keen to have alone time that I had taken to long walks around town. I recognized the trees on this street, the homeowner's association had been very clear about how these trees were to be trimmed so the street was distinctive enough for me to remember it after all these years.

"We aren't that far away from my mom's house. How far away is the storage unit from there?" I asked.

"I think it's a couple of miles. We are going to have to power walk to get there, I don't know how long it will be before the police catch on and get the owner to open it up for them, so we should hurry," Ryan said. *A couple of miles?* It wasn't a hot day, thankfully, but with Quin insisting that I carry him, I soon got warm.

I had tried to suggest taking a bus, but Ryan pointed out that buses all have cameras on board now and we would be filmed. We were trying to act as though we hadn't been here at all. Ryan said he had managed to put a spell on his license plate to make it hard for roadside cameras to read, but as his car was at his house, we hadn't been able to use it to get here.

I had to assume that we were all under suspicion. The police would be making sure Ryan and I weren't trying to hide any evidence, so we had to act cautiously. We were trying to *find* evidence though; it probably just wouldn't sound believable if they caught us.

By the time we made it to the parking lot of the storage place, I was sweaty and feeling ready to hit the hay. Quin seemed unphased by the level of inconvenience he had caused by refusing to walk, and had also refused to let Ryan carry him, meaning that Ryan wasn't quite as hot and didn't have aching arms from holding them in a strange position for nearly an hour.

It seemed that there wasn't a security guard onsite, just a few well-placed cameras to keep an eye over the entire facility.

"Operculum," Ryan whispered. I saw the clear glass of the cameras turn black as if they had been covered in spray paint. This should buy us enough time to have a look before anyone notices. We walked across the parking lot, Quin now happy to be on his feet, and navigated through the maze of pathways until we found number 42.

I leaned against the wall that separated the doors between this unit and number 43 beside it, fantasizing about climbing into bed and sleeping for two days. My eye lids fell heavy over my eyes, my head nodding forward as I drifted into a standing sleep. The sound of the garage door rolling back into the roof of the unit startled me and I stepped away from the bricks, turned and looked at the contents of Lee's storage unit.

It was somehow organized and chaotic in equal measure. There were shelving units around the edges where he had obviously had good intentions about keeping this place neat, then it had descended into piles of boxes on the floor. There were also a few trash bags to the left that looked full, the whole place had a scent of vanilla and green juice, it's a distinctive smell that anyone who has ever drank celery juice would recognize.

I was drawn to the trash bags for some reason, they were very loosely knotted as if the intention had always been to be able to get back into them easily. When I opened the bag I could see a huge amount of powder, the vanilla and green juice scent flooding my senses.

"These boxes are open, but just all filled with canisters of Nutraspin," Ryan said, peering into a box that had been slashed open with a box cutter.

"Are some of them empty? The canisters I mean. This bag is filled with milkshake powder, or at least that's what I think it is. Why would he dump out the product he is trying to sell?" I asked.

I watched Ryan unscrew the lid on one of the canisters and could see from where I was stood that there was no plastic seal across the top, this was one of the containers that Lee had emptied. Ryan reached inside and pulled out roll after roll of cash, wrapped tightly and secured with an elastic band. What had been happening in here? Why did Lee have so much money?

9

It isn't a good sign that someone is hiding enormous roles of money, never mind the fact that same someone has been murdered. Ryan was working his way through the open boxes and trying to see how many of the Nutraspin canisters were filled with rolls of cash, then doing some mental math to figure out how much was hidden in here.

I was still tired, but the adrenaline of the find was like a shot of caffeine and I felt able to carry on. Quin had curled up on one of the sealed boxes and seemed as though he didn't have a care in the world. You wouldn't think we were in the middle of a murder investigation with how loudly he was purring in his sleep.

I was still waiting. "I opened up one of the rolls, they are all twenty dollar bills and there seems to be one hundred of them in each roll. That means each of these rolls is two thousand dollars. This seems like a money laundering set up," Ryan explained.

"What? That seems like something that big-time criminals do, right? Lee was just cheating himself, he was paying for product and pretending he was selling it on to customers when he wasn't," I exclaimed.

"Nora, come on. Where would all this money be coming from

otherwise?" he said. I didn't have an answer. Lee was in the red on every account we had looked at, he had spent all the savings, put them in danger of losing their home, but was somehow still scraping together enough to pay the utility bills to keep the lights on. He had gotten involved in a pyramid scheme in a moment of desperation, had he been caught up in something even worse after that?

"Money laundering, I don't even know how that works. Is it related to the milkshakes? I don't get it," I muttered, struggling to comprehend how Lee had kept all this from my mom.

"Possibly, in which case my workload is about to get even crazier. Someone will be engaging in an illegal activity, let's say selling illicit substances. That is a cash-only business. In order to spend it that money would need to be 'cleaned' so that it doesn't raise suspicion from the cops. Maybe you buy a legitimate business like a laundromat and then give your 'dirty' money to a few dozen people that then come into the laundromat and put it into the machines for you.

"That would be a slow way to 'clean' thousands of dollars, but at least that business is earning, what looks like, a legitimate income. Obviously it would be sketchy if the owner of a laundromat was driving around in a Lamborghini. Maybe they own a casino, that would be an easier way to move this amount of cash around," Ryan sighed.

I spotted something on the ground, just barely poking out from beneath the shelving rack I was leaning against. I bent down and picked it up. It was a chip from a casino in town, Ryan must have been right. I turned the chip over and over in my fingers, as if I was trying to will it all not to be true, but the evidence was pointing us in a very clear direction.

"Sky Roller," I said. I passed him the chip. "It's a place in town that I've been past a few times, as far as I know it's the only one around. I didn't even think Lee liked to gamble, but he was clearly into taking risks and managed to keep that a secret from us."

"Okay, well we should check that place out. This unit is filled with unsold milkshake powder and money, so I think we've learned all we need to. Look, you are clearly too exhausted to transport the three of us back to Sucré, and I can't do that kind of magic. If we want to check out the casino then we are better doing it later, at a normal time for people to visit.

"I know a place nearby where we can stay, it's a hotel that caters to a lot of magic folk. They won't tell the police we've been there so there's no need to worry about leaving a trail," he said, stroking the side of my face. He weaved his way between the boxes to come over and give me a hug and I hadn't realized how much I needed it until he was wrapped around me.

"Okay," I managed. Ryan gave Quin a nudge and we left the storage unit. Before we closed the door, Ryan whispered something quietly and a dot of light rushed from his fingers and began to twirl around the piles of boxes and the floor, anywhere that we had touched.

"That should take care of fingerprints and any other traces we might have left, it's a new spell I found in an old book. Come on." He wrapped his arm around my body, allowing me to lean on him slightly as we walked out of the labyrinth of units and back out to the parking lot. I wasn't paying enough attention to follow the directions, but I could see Quin trotting along beside me as we walked over an endless sidewalk, turning left and right.

By the time we reached the hotel I felt briefly revived, the fresh air had helped, but my magic felt depleted and it was a type of fatigue I hadn't experienced before. Perhaps with more practice at the transportation spell I would be able to get from one town and another without being useless for the rest of the day.

"Two adults, one cat," Ryan said to the woman behind the counter. The fact that she didn't question why we were trying to book a cat into a hotel was the first sign that this place was different. The lights floating in midair was another. Lamps of all shapes and sizes hovering above the ground like a magical art installation. They all suddenly dropped onto flat surfaces as someone walked out of an elevator, I wondered if that person had been human and the magic here was supposed to be a secret.

"Thank you, you're in room fifteen, just take the elevator up two floors and you'll find it, probably," she instructed. We walked over to the elevator and pressed the button for the next floor up. After a few seconds the lift doors opened again, and the view had changed. It didn't feel as though we had moved at all, yet now we were in a different place.

The room opposite the elevator was room twelve, which led me to believe that thirteen would be right next door. No. Next to room twelve was room twenty-eight. Then four. I don't know why witches insist on making things more complicated for their own amusement, but I was so tired that I didn't have the energy to hunt for the right place.

Sleeping on the carpet of the corridor was getting more tempting by the second, but Ryan shouted that he had found the right door and I staggered in the direction of his voice. He opened the door and revealed a room with floor to ceiling windows along the far wall, milky light filtered through sheer white curtains and gave the room a golden glow.

Quin ran past my leg to curl up on the cat bed that was waiting in the corner beside a bowl of milk and some treats. It was as if the room was made up of all of our fantasy hotel rooms. The bed was huge, the pillows plump and inviting. I could see from the doorway that the duvet was heavy and soft, I ran towards it, the sheets pulled back as I leapt through the air and landed gently onto the mattress.

Ryan came over to pull the covers over me and I was asleep before he had chance to shut the curtains. I fell into a deep sleep that was restorative, even in my dreams I could feel my magic coming back to me. I dreamt of the storage unit, of the rolls of cash hidden in the containers and the thought of my mom in a jail miles away from here. I woke up suddenly and saw that Ryan was gone.

The sun was no longer pouring through the glass and I had to assume it was night now. Quin was purring gently in the corner and I sat up to look around the room. I had been so tired when I got here that I hadn't realized just how big this place was. I wondered how much this had cost. There was a kitchenette and I spotted a takeout container on the counter. I wriggled free from the sheets and walked over, the bag was still warm.

I opened it up and was hit by the smell of the Chinese food inside, it had been so tightly contained in the paper bag that I hadn't known what it was. Opening up the cartons I could see spring rolls, Chow Mein and a set of chopsticks. Had Ryan just been in here to drop it off, or had the hotel made this appear when I woke up?

Either way, I didn't care. I bundled up the food in my arms and carried it to the balcony, the curtains had pulled themselves apart enough for me to see the door to the outside and it opened as I approached. I sat at the small metal table and leaned back in the chair as I ate, appreciating a view of the town that I had never seen before.

I heard Ryan come back into the hotel room, I turned to wave to him to join me outside. He grabbed a second take out bag that had appeared on the kitchen counter next to mine and wandered out into the evening air, sitting across from me and beginning to eat.

"Where have you been?" I asked.

"I wanted to check out the casino, just to have a quick look from the outside to see if I could spot anything obvious. I'm still trying to understand how Lee could have gotten tied up with them. I can't help thinking that they came across him through the pyramid scheme somehow," he sighed.

"Did you spot anything?"

"No, it all looks pretty regular. They aren't going to be driving around with big dollar signs on the side of black vans though are they. He must have been physically meeting up with someone, somehow, and this was how the dirty money was put into his hands. Either that or they had a secret drop off spot and he would collect it alone. We need to speak to your mom, but that's not super easy right now," he said, lifting his chopsticks and noodles to his mouth.

"Do you think my mom knew about the cash?" I asked. I didn't know what I expected him to say, there was no way of knowing that yet. Would she even tell me the truth if I asked her? "Wait, mom said she thought he was having an affair. Did you see any emails that back that up?"

"I didn't read all that many of them, just the ones about the storage unit and the orders he was putting in with his supervisor. I mean, there were so many I'd have to go back and look again. The computer is at your place," he said, sitting up a little straighter. "What are you thinking?"

"If he was messaging somebody about meeting up, maybe that was for the money handover. Not an affair, but part of this money laundering thing. If you didn't know about the cash, then reading those emails might lead you to believe he was cheating. We need to go through his inbox first thing tomorrow. I think if I get another round of sleep after this casino trip then I should have the strength to use my transportation magic in the morning," I said, feeling confident that I was on the right track.

Now we just had the small matter of walking into the casino, which may very well be the lion's den of criminal activity. We suspected that these people might have been involved in Lee's murder and we were about to be surrounded by them. Outnumbered and underprepared perhaps, but I'd just had Chinese for breakfast.

It was time to go.

1 0

The inside of the casino had been what I had expected, a series of dimly lit spaces filled with slot machines and tables for playing higher stakes games. If anything suspicious was happening in here, then it would be happening at those tables. No one would be laundering money in silver dollars in the fruit machines but buying chips with a roll of twenties would work.

I had taken the chip from the ground in the storage unit and brought it with me, Ryan still went to the teller behind the bullet proof class and traded in some of his own money for a stack of chips and then returned to me.

"I assume we are looking for someone regular that is spending a ton of money, right?" I asked.

"Yeah, I guess the name of the game is camouflage. The person laundering the money will just be some regular looking person, not too flashy but not obviously broke, otherwise that would raise suspicion," he replied.

"Doesn't somebody check the books? Like an authority or something?" I said, smoothing down the evening dress that had been hanging in the hotel wardrobe.

"If they start being reckless with it then yeah, but if they are doing it carefully then they could get away with it for months at a time, maybe even a year before the FBI get involved. That dirty money is coming from somewhere, they would have federal accountants that help crack down on crime this way, by investigating large cash transactions," he explained. "Come on."

We walked over to the poker table closest to us and took two empty seats. I hadn't played this game before, especially not while doing some undercover investigative work, so I was already feeling nervous. Ryan seemed to have some experience with the game and began placing bets and tapping the table to communicate with the dealer to put down another card.

Free drinks were distributed by a team of smiling, uniformed staff and I could see why people would want to spend so much time in here. After his third drink, Ryan excused himself to find the bathroom and I was left alone at the table.

"Ma'am, you can't sit at the table unless you play," the dealer explained.

"Oh, okay," I nodded, pushing over a couple of Ryan's chips and beginning a new game. I managed to win a few hands which gave me the confidence, or perhaps the adrenaline, to carry on. Somehow only a few rounds later basically all my chips were gone. Gambling really wasn't for me.

I remembered the chip in my purse and fished it out to place another bet. The dealer picked it up in his hands and turned it over. Then I saw him reach underneath the table and before I knew it, two security guards were lifting me up beneath each arm and taking me through a door marked 'staff only'.

I asked them over and over what was happening, but neither of them would speak. How would Ryan find me back here? Was I in trouble? Did they somehow know where I had gotten it from? A man walked into the room and one of the guards left, this didn't feel like a good thing.

"My name is Charlie, I assume you are Nora Wildes," he said. My mouth fell open in astonishment, how could he know my name? All I could muster was a nod of acknowledgment and then he continued to speak. "Well, Nora. I believe your stepfather is dead now, a shame to be sure." He hung his head for a moment and then looked up at me, the commiserating expression now gone. "Something you should know about me is that I run a very tight ship around here."

"I see that," I whimpered.

"I know if things go missing, I see when people take things they shouldn't take. I know that our now dearly departed Lee Jackson took casino property and that you have decided to return it today. Why did you do that, Nora?"

"The chip?" I asked. He nodded. Charlie sat down behind a large desk and reclined in his office chair, somehow this pretense of calm made me feel more frightened. "I found it," I replied.

"And where did you find it?" he asked, suddenly sitting forward with both of his elbows resting on the mahogany table between us. I knew better than to answer this, because if I told him that I found it among the boxes full of money that he was forcing my stepfather to launder through the casino then I would be trapped in the same situation that had gotten Lee killed.

Ryan walked into the room, looked at the two of us, then reached to lift me up from the chair. "Ah, Mr. Hughes, nice of you to come *inside* the casino. Did you enjoy your tour of the parking lot earlier?" Charlie grinned.

"We are going now, thanks for giving her the VIP experience," Ryan grunted.

"You'll be seeing me," Charlie said, smiling so widely that all of his teeth were showing. It was like a shark right before the attack, I could sense the danger without any threats being made aloud.

We walked out of the office and straight back to the parking lot outside. Ryan had already ordered us a taxi somehow and we were soon driving away from the building in silence.

"Well I think that answers the question as to whether something shady is going on," I laughed. It was one of those moments where you can either laugh or cry, so I tried to find the silver lining. The guy who ran the casino knew Lee by name, that had to mean something. I had assumed we were headed back to the hotel, but we pulled up outside a bakery instead. Despite the time it was still open.

Ryan hadn't said much on the short journey over, but I suspected he was contemplating the amount of work this would mean if he could have it added to his case against the pyramid scheme company. He paid the driver and we stepped out, the air heavy with the smell of imminent rain and cinnamon.

"I looked up a cute place that we could eat at so late, turns out this bakery has the highest reviews of anywhere in town," he grinned. He took my hand and guided me onto the sidewalk, navigating my heeled feet over the puddles from the previous storm.

It wasn't bright inside, the twinkling string lights across the ceiling made a sky of stars for us to sit beneath. There wasn't a hard-wooden seat or stool to be found, only deep sofas and cushioned bar chairs. It was like visiting a friend's house, the only other customers in the building smiled as we entered and we were waved in by a woman behind the cash register.

"Two hot chocolates please, we'll take any extras you've got!" Ryan grinned. "Marshmallows, whipped cream… all of it!"

"Coming right up," the woman replied. We took a spot that was slightly separated from the rest of the café. It reminded me of a camp-fire glow, a small candle on the table in front of us adding an extra sparkle.

"You don't seem concerned about that guy," Ryan said.

"Will worrying make anything change?" I asked. He smiled and shrugged his shoulders.

"Good point. I vote we don't go back to the casino."

"Ha, yeah obviously," I smirked. "I think we made a great first impression and we should quit while we are ahead."

"Two hot chocolates," the woman announced as she carried them over on a tray. They were fully loaded, the drink stopped probably two inches below the peak of the whipped cream and there were fudge pieces, marshmallows and a couple of cookies on the saucer for dipping. The whole thing had been drizzled with a thick chocolate sauce and I already wanted a second one.

We laughed as we realized that the music being played was just called 'ski-lodge ambiance' as the waitress changed over the track on the CD player. It felt worlds away from the place we had been only an hour before.

"Do you think you might have the strength to summon Lee's laptop here? I hate to ask, but I really want to get this sorted as quickly as possible and—"

"Sure," I interrupted. I wanted my mom out of jail and Ryan wanted to see everyone involved brought to justice. I turned my back on the rest of the café and whispered, "Devoco". The laptop appeared in my hands and I turned back around to place it down on the table next to the candle.

Ryan opened it up and went straight for the email inbox, searching through the dozens of order confirmations and payment receipts from Nutraspin. Scattered throughout were messages that didn't have the same subject titles as the others. When Ryan clicked on one, we read through it quickly.

'Lee,

I can't wait to see you again. Thank you for the flowers, they really brighten up the place. See you in room four tomorrow.

C'

Were these the messages that my mom had seen? She had suspected him of having an affair and these emails sure sounded like they were sent between two people keeping secrets. Or was this related to the money exchange? It was all getting so confusing that I slouched back against the sofa cushions and polished off my hot chocolate.

"Well, saying a room number like that suggests they are meeting in a hotel. There is only one hotel nearby that secretive people would go to," Ryan sighed.

"The one we are staying at?"

"Exactly. There are two other hotels in town but they are both part of big chains, our hotel is discreet. It's run by witches and they understand that sometimes people need to travel undetected. I would bet that this is the hotel where this 'C' had been meeting with Lee."

"Are you thinking 'C' could stand for Charlie?" I asked.

"I'd like to hope not. If he was meeting with the casino boss and not some lower down stooge, then we might be treading on some toes by looking into this." I could see Ryan's brow furrowing deeper, he didn't want to get us both into danger and we both knew that we might have to expose our magic to humans if we were cornered.

The sound of someone landing on the ground caused me to whip my head round to see what had caused the noise. A woman had tripped over on her way out and was desperately scrambling back onto her feet. She looked at me, incredibly briefly, from beneath the brim of her hat and, once she was upright, bolted for the door. She hadn't picked up everything she had dropped.

She been pretty close to us when she had tripped, so I could see what she had left behind, all scattered across the tiles. Two things in particular stood out to me. The first was a key with a number engraved into it. The key was old, cast iron and comically heavy. I left the sofa to pick up the stuff in the vague hope of returning it all to her, but she was long gone.

Who would ever need such a heavy key? There were also a couple of poker chips from 'Sky Roller'. The chips felt most concerning. I carried everything over to Ryan and sat back down to show him what I had collected.

We obviously knew from Charlie's reaction that he considered it a terrible sin to remove casino property from the building, so this woman was already in trouble. I showed Ryan the key and he reached into his suit pocket and retrieved one that was almost identical, but nowhere near as heavy. The key Ryan was holding had, 'fifteen' etched into the loop near the top. The one I was holding had 'four'.

This was the key to room four of the hotel we were staying at, the very same room that Lee had been having secret meetings with 'C'. Was this person about to do something illegal? What worried me most is that, when I caught a glimpse of her face, I could have sworn it was Molly from the café back in Sucré.

If she was heading back to the hotel now, then we would need to leave quickly in order to catch up. All of the relaxed feeling that I'd had in the bakery had quickly left and I was stuck wondering why on earth Molly would be here. Had I seen her in the stranger's face by mistake? Molly had a business back in Sucré, as far as I knew all of her family lived there too, why would she be in *this* town at this hour?

I wasn't sure if Ryan had seen her face too, so I couldn't ask him to confirm what I had seen. We seemed to have a silent understanding that we were involving ourselves in returning this key, that we needed to see who it had belonged to and what was happening in that hotel room. When we were standing on the sidewalk, we could see the brake lights of the taxi she must have taken. She was ahead of us by a few hundred feet and heading in the direction of the hotel.

Ryan hailed a passing cab and asked the driver to drop us off at the delivery entrance for the hotel. If we were to step out by the main entrance then we would risk being spotted, this way allowed us to stay hidden.

We strapped ourselves into the back and the taxi pulled away, the acceleration forcing us back against the leather seats. Was I *hoping* that it was Molly? I didn't like the idea that she was caught up in this messy world, but what could I do about it if she was?

We turned one corner, then another. All the while I stayed silent as I thought about walking into that flower shop and seeing Herb's face, the horror of realizing what had happened to Lee. Was Molly at risk of being murdered too? The streetlights strobed as we passed them at speed, flooding the taxi with light, then complete darkness falling over us again.

"Whatever happens, Molly was okay five minutes ago. We are doing everything we can," Ryan reassured. He had seen her too.

"We don't know what we are about to walk in on," I said, my head still fixed on the view rushing by as we turned onto the street of the hotel. We didn't take the regular route, at some point the taxi driver turned right and drove through a set of iron gates that separated the parking lot from the street. "We want to stay hidden, right? At what point do we intervene? How will we know when to make ourselves known?"

"We'll know," Ryan said solemnly.

We stepped out of the cab and ran back to the iron gates, tucking ourselves behind them so as not to block the exit as the car turned and drove back through them. The driver gave us a nod, then sped away into the distance. We were alone here now, the sound of a stray cat howling from the other side of the lot caused me to flinch, but Ryan grabbed my hand and we began to approach the back of the hotel.

"Look," he said. "The door isn't closed all the way." He was right, there was a fire door that was propped open. It looked accidental, gravel from a dedicated smoker's area seemed to have been kicked along the path and some had settled right by the door frame. Whoever had last tried to close it didn't seem to have noticed that it wasn't properly shut.

I stepped closer and put the tips of my fingers along the edge of the door. It wasn't open much, but there was just enough surface to grab that I could pull it open. We were looking in at the hotel kitchen. It was less industrial that I would have expected, there wasn't a stainless still countertop in sight. It seemed more like a home from home.

My own kitchen frequently redecorated itself, it had been every color under the sun over the last twelve months, but this felt oddly familiar. There was no one else in the kitchen except me and Ryan, no staff to bust us breaking in. We walked towards the lit hallway across the room and came out opposite a janitor's closet. We could hear the reception staff talking to someone and saw a figure rush by us.

By the time we had gotten close enough to the desk the reception area was quiet. Whoever they had been speaking to must have gone. Ryan parted his lips as if to speak and the two women behind their computers looked up at him in preparation to answer his question, but he thought better of it. He knew they wouldn't give out personal information about another guest.

We had guessed that room four would be on the next floor up, so we gave an acknowledging smile to both of them and walked over to the elevator. We pushed the call button and the doors immediately opened. We stepped in, Ryan pressed the silver circle with '1' glowing in its center, and in the blink of an eye the doors opened again and we were in a new place.

"I'll go left, you go right," I suggested. "Don't worry, if you hear me screaming then you can just come running!" I laughed. Ryan wasn't in the mood for jokes.

"What if you are outnumbered? What if…"

"Calm down, this hotel isn't so big that you couldn't get to me quickly. We are both heading for the same room so it's not like you won't know where I am. Look, room four could be anywhere along this corridor, it will save time if we split up and we can find Molly faster. Go!" I prompted.

I turned on my heels and began power walking along the beige carpet, looking left and right quickly to inspect the numbers on the doors. A door just behind me opened, someone reached out and pulled me backwards into the room. I tried to take a breath so that I could shout for Ryan, but before I knew it the door had closed behind me and I was standing face to face with Molly.

"Mo—what are you doing here?" I stuttered.

"Keep your voice down!" she warned.

"This isn't room four," I whispered back.

"No, this is my room. I seem to have lost the key that I needed and I am freaking out," she gasped. I thought about the key she had dropped and remembered that it was currently sitting in Ryan's pocket.

It seemed that she was halfway through packing and there was a half-filled suitcase on the hotel bed. The only light was coming from a small desk lamp but I could see the worry in the shadows across her face. Why was she so nervous?

"Are you going to tell me what's going on?" I asked. She slumped onto the bed beside her suitcase and I pulled the chair from beneath the desk so that I could sit across from her. She ran her hands through her hair and then looked up at me.

"I heard about a new way to make some extra money on the side. I had always dreamed of retiring early and travelling but running a café makes it hard to put thousands of dollars into a savings account. I just about turn a profit most months," she said.

"Is this because of the cat café?" I asked. I felt a pang of guilt that Quin had set up a business across the street from her own that had stolen some of her customers.

"No, it's been like this for years. I actually got a boost when you opened that place, more people were coming to the area and it meant that for a few months I had extra cash that I wanted to invest with, you know, have my money work for me. You see people on TV all the time that buy stocks and shares in something and then they can make their millions from the comfort of their sofa," she smiled.

"You've invested in something?" I asked, wondering if she had bought shares in the casino or something.

"I invested in myself, or at least that's how it was sold to me. Have you heard of Nutraspin?" she asked. I felt my heart sink. I nodded but struggled to hide the concern from my face. "Ah, you know more than I did when I got involved then. I suppose for some people it's easier to spot a multi-level marketing scheme but I was naïve. I was told that I could work for myself and set my own hours, selling products of such a high quality that it would almost sell itself."

"Did you end up buying stock you couldn't sell?" I said.

"Yes, and when I started reaching out to others in the forums, I realized just how common that is. I know of people that have gotten into worse situations than me, I only bought a few surplus boxes and they fit in my garage. One of the guys online said he had a whole storage unit full," she sighed.

My pulse raced. She was talking about Lee, right? How many other men would have gotten themselves into that exact situation?

"My stepdad was involved in Nutraspin," I began. "He... well he did a lot of ordering and not a lot of selling. His name was Lee Jackson."

"Lee? That's your stepdad? Wasn't he kil—"

"Killed? Yes. That's why we are here, Ryan and I. He had bought so much milkshake stuff that he was massively in the debt, we think he borrowed money from the wrong kind of people and now he's dead. Do you know anything about that? I think you were talking to him online," I said, the desperation in my voice was clear.

"Nora, all I know is that someone that was posting anonymously said they had bought dozens and dozens of boxes. Maybe over a hundred, I don't know for sure. I can show you what he posted, but he didn't put much personal information on there. I remember him saying he had platinum status and that he was gunning for the all-expenses paid trip to Jamaica. The person in our region that sold the most would win the vacation, he said he wanted to surprise his wife."

He wanted to win a trip for my mom and him, this was probably *slightly* cheaper than paying for the trip by himself, so he was buying more and more to seem like a great salesman. He was already in so much debt though, how could he afford to buy any more of the stuff?

"What do you know about Sky Roller?" I asked.

"You've met Charlie?" she replied. I nodded. "He's my brother, it's nothing to worry about. I came out here to visit him. I know he can be intimidating but..." she trailed off. "I should really get going anyway, it was great to see you and there will be a huge coffee with your name on it the next time you pop by the café. On me of course."

I smiled and took my cue to leave. Something had changed since I brought up the casino but I couldn't sense what it was. The suggestion was that she had the casino chip because her brother owned the place, but did I believe her? She was trapped in the pyramid scheme too and I wanted to help her get out before something terrible happened. I walked out of the room and made my way back towards the elevator hoping to find Ryan there. I didn't know just how much danger Molly was in.

12

Waking up every hour or so through the night left me drained. Ryan and Quin patiently sat through my break down of the events with Molly, and by that I mean Quin would let me speak for almost fifteen seconds at a time without interrupting. I had fallen asleep on top of the bed sheets from exhaustion. Anxiety woke me frequently though, and at five in the morning I gave up hope of getting any more rest.

I walked to the bathroom of the hotel suite and assessed my reflection. I was so close to completing my magic studies and getting the restrictions on my powers lifted, maybe if I had graduated already then I would have been able to transport us back to Sucré without delay, instead of waiting for my magic to recharge.

I looked at the amber streak across my left eye, it seemed brighter now than I had ever seen it. I felt a sudden urge to check in with Molly. I had been thinking about the conversations with Lee that she had mentioned, maybe there were more clues hidden in those messages than she realized and they could help me get to the bottom of all this.

I quickly brushed my teeth, then crept out of the hotel room as silently as I could. Quin flinched a few times at the sound of my footsteps on the creaky floorboards, but he didn't wake up, so I left unnoticed. The elevator rose from the ground floor and the door opened quietly, it was as if the hotel knew I was trying to travel without disturbing any sleeping guests.

I had looked back at the door when I walked out of Molly's room last night to check the room number, so knew where I was headed. I knocked gently against the wood of number seven but there was no answer. She was probably still sleeping. I knocked again, still nothing.

I wrapped my hands around the door handle and whispered, 'resigno!', but this didn't unlock the door as I had been expecting. One of the hotel staff that had been sitting behind the desk was suddenly by my side and let out a deep sigh of annoyance as if I had woken her. It turned out that I had.

"Ma'am, you can't break into people's rooms in this hotel. We have magic that stops it being possible, you know this place puts discretion above all else," she moaned. She yawned and her eyes looked a little puffy, my attempt at an 'unlock' spell had clearly been a trigger for her to respond and she was called from her bed.

"I'm sorry, I just wanted to check on my friend. Her name is Molly, she is in this room and I was talking with her last night, I'm worried about her. That's all," I explained. It was true, but not the whole truth. I was worried about her but didn't think that she was in any immediate danger. I wanted her to show me the forums where people were discussing their involvement with Nutraspin. I wanted to learn everything I could about Lee.

"Molly, eh? Well, how do I know that you aren't an assassin that is trying to bust into her room to kill her. Hmm? Well?" the woman pressed.

"Wouldn't I have a weapon with me or something?" I replied.

"You're a witch aren't you? You *are* a weapon." She had a point.

"Look, she seemed scared last night and I think something was bothering her. She is involved in a pyramid scheme, and that…"

"Say no more. Pyramid scheme? Those things are dangerous all right. Look, I'll let you in but I'm coming in with you. No funny business, ya hear?" she said, thrusting a stern finger towards my face as if scolding a child. I nodded in compliance and she pulled a key from her back pocket, gave me another glare to assess if I was really going to behave myself, then unlocked the door.

The room was empty. Completely and totally empty. Obviously the furniture was still there, but all of Molly's belongings, the suitcase contents that had been strewn about so wildly when I had been here last night and the packets of candy that she had planned to binge eat, were gone.

"Hmm," the woman said. She clicked her fingers and a digital tablet appeared in her hands, she began scrolling through some sort of database and tutting as she read. "It doesn't look like she checked out with any of the staff at the desk, but she has a room booked here for two more nights. Maybe she had an early start this morning." She shrugged but I had a bad feeling about it.

Something I had said last night had spooked her, when we had mentioned the casino, mentioned her brother, she changed. Now she was gone. This didn't feel right. I thanked the woman for her help, she double checked that I was in fact a guest at the hotel and not a spy from a rival business, then I made my way back to my room.

Ryan and Quin were awake now and debating something utterly trivial as per usual.

"Quin, why would I make it up? They don't sell eggs in the refrigerator sections of grocery stores in the UK. They don't wash the eggs before they pack them, it's something about avoiding the transmission of salmonella from the outside to the inside of the egg. I didn't make the policy, it's just how it is," Ryan ranted.

"Ryan, please. I highly doubt that there is a single thing about chicken eggs that I don't know, and I laugh in the face of you telling me that British eggs are any different to American eggs. Do you think the little British hens are walking around in a fancy hat with a cane? Reading Shakespeare and going to watch theatre productions? If their eggs aren't refrigerated, then where are they? On a shelf? Please..." Quin scoffed.

"As important as this conversation clearly is, we need to get back to Sucré. Now," I instructed. "I can get us back; I feel strong enough."

I didn't think that we had been as 'under the radar' as planned. The whole reason we didn't take our cars to and from this town was so that the police wouldn't be able to trace our movements, but given that we got into a conversation with the casino owner, I'd spoken to a staff member at the hotel *and* I'd spoken with Molly, it wouldn't be hard to follow the lead if anyone gave information to the police.

If they thought that we were investigating my stepdad's murder independently, which we were, then they would have reason to suspect that we were planning to hide any evidence we found. My mom was currently locked up for allegedly killing her husband and we were looking for answers, I just hoped that we could find the truth before the police intervened and put a stop to our search.

"It's actually a matter of principle that you defend the American Egg industry, Ryan. Don't think that this conversation is over just because we have to run off to deal with *another* crisis. You are unpatriotic, and I for one will not stand—" Quin was interrupted by my hand scooping him up from the ground. I grabbed onto Ryan's arm and we disappeared in an instant, the cool air rushing past the three of us until we landed on our feet in the hallway of my Sucré home.

"There you are!" Edith cheered. The ghost of my aunt was floating in the hallway mirror, beaming at the sight of me as if she had been desperate to tell me something for days. Quin ran off to find the other cats and Ryan staggered towards the kitchen to make us both a coffee. I slumped down onto the bottom step of the staircase in preparation for a long story from Edith.

"Here I am," I confirmed.

"Any update about my sister?" she asked. As hard as it was for me to see my own mother in handcuffs, it must have been even harder for Edith. Her sister had been arrested and she was in no position to offer any help. She was dead, trapped in the mirrors and unable to interact with the rest of the world unless I facilitated it. Of course, she wanted to help out, but she couldn't.

"Not yet, I will call the station in a few hours. It's too early for anyone important to be in the office yet. I need to find her a full-time lawyer, and—"

"I'll defend her!" Ryan hollered from the kitchen.

"Well," I laughed. "That's one thing to cross off my to-do list. Look, I need to find Molly, get her to speak to help me build a timeline for the morning of the murder and then we can work on getting that information to the police. The window of opportunity for this murder is mere minutes, if we can prove that mom was in the café when it occurred then she might be let out."

"Why do you look so worried then?" Edith asked.

"Molly is… well I don't know how reliable of a witness she will be. There seems to be a lot of other stress going on, she is tied up in Nutraspin too. I just want to see what she can remember from that morning, maybe she has a time stamp on the cash register that shows when we arrived, or CCTV cameras or something," I sighed.

"You'll figure it out. You always do," Edith smiled. I felt encouraged, obviously the motivation to carry on was that I didn't want to sit back and watch my mom go to prison for years over something I was certain she hadn't done.

"Do you know where Molly lives?" I asked loudly, hoping that Ryan could hear me too.

"I thought she lived off Elm Avenue, or maybe on the other side of town past the events hall," Ryan answered. He had brought through a mug of coffee and handed it to me, leaning against the door frame as he drank his own. "There will be someone in the bakery by now anyway, they start so early to do… bread things."

"Bread things?" I chuckled. "Yeah, you're right. I'll walk over now and see if she is there, or maybe someone else would be able to tell me where to find her."

I drank my coffee, rubbing my temples in between sips like I was revving up my mental engine for the day. "I will walk with you, I can head into the office and sort out taking your mom as a client so that I can be her defense lawyer in this case. Not to mention the bigger case with Nutraspin. Oh gosh, I can picture the pile of paperwork already," Ryan smirked.

"Thank you for looking out for us," I said. "It means a lot that you trust my instinct that my mom is innocent."

"Of course I trust you. Your family is my family," he replied, stepping forward to sit beside me on the stairs and kissing me on the shoulder. We *were* one family. I felt a shiver of excitement as I recalled the vision I'd had of our wedding, but didn't want to dwell in the fantasy for too long as I had business to take care of.

As we left the house, I shouted a goodbye to Quin and then started to walk at great speed up the street. Ryan was feigning the need to jog in order to keep up, but I wanted to speak to Molly as soon as possible. She had information that I needed, I was sure of it.

We parted ways on the high street and I ran to the café. Molly wasn't there. The woman who had warned me away from Molly's business ideas was rushing about in the kitchen area and came to the door when she saw me. She had hastily applied her name badge and it sat wonky across her chest; Rebecca.

"Nora, have you seen Molly anywhere?" she asked. I shook my head. "She was supposed to open up this morning with me, but I can't get hold of her. I have never known her to miss a day of work, something must have happened." I gulped nervously. Molly was missing.

13

$\mathcal{R}$ebecca invited me inside and locked the door behind us. The rising sun was flooding the sky with an orange-pink glow, like a watercolor painting, and it filtered into the café to create new shadows. Rebecca walked into the back of the kitchen and returned with a cup of tea for both of us. As she sat across from me I was able to see the deep lines across her forehead, as if she had lived a life full of surprise and worry. I had no doubt my face would have similar wrinkles soon.

"What do you think has happened?" she asked.

"You told me not to get involved with her business idea, did you know what it was when you said that?" I replied.

"She got hooked on Nutraspin. I assume you know that now," she began. I nodded. "Look, she gave me the sales pitch too, even offered me a free sample of the stuff. I'm all for a free sample, let me tell you, but it wasn't a 'no strings attached' situation. I drank the stuff for a week, even offered to buy myself some and help her out. I felt as though my skin was a little brighter and I had more energy so I figured maybe there was something to it.

"I felt like making sales wasn't what she wanted to do. She seemed determined to get me on board as an employee, recruit me to sell health shakes to other people. I quickly realized that this was a pyramid scheme and when I said as much to her, well, she got upset."

"You didn't want to sign up?" I asked. Involvement in a scheme like this often came from a combination of naivety and desperation. Molly had never stuck me as having either of those traits, she had always seemed too self-assured and she had never mentioned any financial goals to me, or that the café wasn't giving her everything she needed. I was still surprised by it all.

"No, I know plenty of people that have gone around trying to sell low-quality make-up or weird perfumes and they always end up spending more money than they earn. Look, I have had my fair share of money troubles, but I've been reading all these books about personal finance recovery and so many of them mention that these 'sure fire money earners' are often about creating money for those above you and sinking into the red. Although, isn't that every job? Making money for the boss," she smirked.

"Did she mention anything about it going well?" I asked.

"No. I don't know exactly when she signed up, but I remember she started running and buying all this shapewear. In hindsight I suspect that she was planning to advertise herself as a Nutraspin success story with 'before and after' photographs even though her weight loss had nothing to do with those stupid shakes. It's all a scam. I've become skeptical of almost everything, I know. Would you like a fresh cinnamon bun?"

The change in topic caught me off guard but as I came out of the daze of the conversation I realized that the room was heavy with the buttery scent of fresh rolls. The smile on my face gave Rebecca her answer and she was soon back at the table with two rolls.

"Do you know where she lives? Maybe she went home and just overslept," I suggested.

"She's never done that. Rumor has it that she had four different alarm clocks scattered around her apartment to make sure she gets to work on time," she smiled. "I've called for another waitress to come in to help out with the breakfast rush, and I can't leave to go and look for her. I won't be getting out of here until at least two o'clock this afternoon."

"I'll go look," I offered. I felt as though whatever had happened to her was my fault. She had been flustered back at that hotel, sure, but something I had done had made her leap into a different type of panic. She had left the hotel in the middle of the night even though she had paid up for two more days, she hadn't even checked out properly. Could her brother, Charlie, have done something? I mentioned his name and she started fidgeting nervously.

Rebecca wrote the address down on a piece of paper towel and I thanked her for breakfast. I recognized the street name and Ryan had been right, she lived just off Elm Avenue. I saw Stacy, the waitress from Quin's café, unlock the doors and seven cats trot in behind her. She gave me a wave when she spotted me and I waved back. The rest of the world was still spinning, even though I had all this to deal with.

My phone started buzzing in my pocket and I answered the call. It was Jeremy, my colleague at the University lab where I worked. I was due in the lab this afternoon and he was probably calling to tell me that all of the cells we had been growing were dead, or something equally annoying. He rarely called with good news.

"Nora?" he said as I picked up.

"Yeah, what's up?" I answered.

"Sorry for the early call, I thought you'd want to know that one of the students had brought in a jar of something blue that they found in their backyard. It is like, it's weird. Super blue. I don't know how else to describe it. They thought we might be able to tell them what it is, I said that we *of course* could tell him, but I literally have no idea. Are you able to come in any earlier today?" he said.

"I have a few things to take care of, so if they don't take too long then I will come in. Have you shown the blue thing to anyone else? Maybe one of the PhD students could help," I suggested.

"Oh they aren't in until nine on the dot. I was just hoping you might be free to rush in and satiate my curiosity. I typed 'weird blue thing' into a search engine and the internet did not help," he chuckled. "I'll see you soon then." Dial tone.

I smiled at the thought of the Professor I worked with hunched over the lab bench staring at a blue thing and a pile of textbooks, desperate to show off to a student that he could find the answer to anything. He should have just shrugged, said 'I don't know' and then he wouldn't be calling me so close to dawn.

By the time I made it to Molly's apartment building, the streets were becoming busy with people making early starts to their work-day. Businesses were opening their shutters, lights flickering on in offices and the hum of slow-moving cars vibrated through the air.

I unlocked the door easily, my magic wasn't blocked here like it was in the hotel. She lived in number three, and with another whisper of, 'Resigno', I was soon inside. Considering that she was running the café and a side business, her house was incredibly clean. She obviously dedicated any spare time she had into keeping her home organized and I couldn't help but feel a twinge of jealousy that she had the motivation.

Unlike Lee, she had a tidy desk space and only a few surplus boxes of Nutraspin. Based on what she had said I doubted that she had a secret storage unit. I wandered quickly from room to room and found no sign of Molly or the suitcase that she had taken to the hotel. She hadn't made it back here. Could she have maybe gone somewhere else instead of Sucré?

Why would Rebecca say she was due back at the café this morning when she had two more nights booked in a town hours away? I went back over to the desk and sat down in her office chair. She had a desktop computer, perfectly dust-free, and with a nudge of the mouse the screen lit up. It wasn't locked and the desktop was visible for me to dive through.

I could see along the task bar that her web browser was already open, clicking on the logo opened up the website she had been on when she was last at her desk. A number of tabs along the top showed the other things she had been looking at.

The first website was the forum for disgruntled Nutraspin recruits. I hadn't heard much about this company until recently, yet there were hundreds of people on this forum discussing the different ways in which they had been screwed over by a supervisor, or the debt that they were now in.

I skimmed through the posts and spotted the user that had mentioned the use of a storage unit for the extra product. I clicked on their profile and could see that this person described the weight of keeping it all a secret from his wife. They talked about the importance of keeping their platinum status and continuing to get the vacations so that it would play into the fantasy life he was building.

Both Molly and Lee, if that was in fact Lee that had posted, talked about their area manager, 'C'. Lee seemed to have had more hostile interactions with 'C', and Molly seemed to be speaking out in defense of this person. It had to be Charlie, right? She was defending her brother, but still seemed to have an issue with the way Nutraspin was treating them.

Molly described 'C' as a reasonable person, and suggested that Lee speak with 'C' and explain the situation he was in. Molly seemed to think that 'C' would ease off and stop putting so much pressure on Lee to sell product, that maybe he would be able to focus on recruitment for a while as that would help him recoup some of his financial losses.

Would Charlie have been calm in the face of an employee asking for a reduced workload? He had seemed hostile at the casino, a control freak that wouldn't cut anyone any slack. Had this prompt from Molly been the beginning of the end for Lee? Had he tried to back out of Nutraspin and angered Charlie? Would Charlie have killed over it?

If my theory was right, then Molly would feel racked with guilt over it. She had pushed Lee into a conversation that he felt uncomfortable having. The phone on the kitchen counter began to ring, but as I was in somewhat of a daze trying to process events, I picked it up. I must have forgotten that this wasn't my house.

"Hello? Is this a relative of a Ms. Molly Wright?" a voice asked.

"Yes," I lied.

"We have Ms. Wright at Immaculate Heart Hospital, her cell phone had this number listed as 'home,'" the voice continued. I felt my stomach sink.

"Is she alive?" I interrupted. There was a silence that felt like an eternity after I asked that question. I could hear the faint sound of hospital address systems requesting that doctors rush to one room or another. Had she been killed too? Was this pyramid scheme a cover up for some mob? This was too much, she was just selling health shakes, how could it have come to this?

"I can't discuss much over the phone for confidentiality reasons, but yes she is alive. I would hurry," the voice replied. My hand was gripping the phone so tightly that the color had drained from my knuckles. The voice confirmed the address for me and I said that I would be there as soon as I could be. I wouldn't be able to just appear in the parking lot, I would have to drive. I rushed out of the apartment, down the stairs and back out onto the sidewalk.

I took a steadying breath and began to run towards Charm Close, I needed to get to my car. I didn't know how bad this all was, I just had to hope that Molly would be okay. She had to be.

I called Ryan to let him know where I was going. I was driving out of Sucré now and had to keep scrolling through the radio stations to find one that was playing music instead of a news bulletin about Lee. It was still the event that every local anchor was talking about as it was unsolved. The buzz of a killer on the loose seemed to draw in more listeners, so it was just an endless loop of re-telling the events of that morning and sound bites from the police.

There had been no update. They had a suspect in custody, that was all they would say. Over and over. My mom was that suspect. They could legally hold you for up to seventy-two hours if they suspected that you had committed a crime, after that they either had to let you go or make a formal arrest. I had no idea what they would decide to do, and neither did the people on the radio.

There seemed to have been a reporter on the streets of Sucré that was asking random residents what they thought of the crime, if they had seen anything and if they felt safe now that the police had someone down at the station. It was all filler, there was nothing to say but they all seemed to want to dwell on it for up to ten minutes at a time. After a second scan through all available stations, I just turned the radio off all together.

Signs for the hospital passed by the car window in a blur. Movement on the back seat made my heart pound and I pulled over. I hadn't checked to see if anyone was hiding in the car, I've seen it happen in movies. I might be a target now, after all my investigation into Nutraspin, the casino and Lee's murder, I might be getting too close to the truth. I whipped my head around, expecting to see Charlie lying flat across the seats with a grin on his face.

"Quin!" I yelled. "I could have had a heart attack!"

"Well, I spotted you crossing the street earlier and I said to myself, *'Quin, you handsome devil you, it looks like Nora is up to something more interesting than sitting in a cat café all day listening to old people complain about crochet hooks',* so I bailed out of work and jumped in your car. I knew you'd end up driving somewhere exciting!" he purred.

"Exciting? I'm going to the hospital, is that exciting?" I replied.

"What are you going there for? I thought you might be heading to that new pet superstore out of town, I saw an ad for it in the middle of my documentary about the zoo the other day. I figured it was just a matter of time until you took me there for some well-deserved cat luxuries." I took a deep breath and tried to remember that I used to actually like cats. Quin was sometimes more of a nuisance than a familiar.

"Are you bored of your café now? You said it was your dream to run a place like that," I said, turning back to face forward and pulling out onto the highway. He leapt onto the passenger seat beside me and curled up into a neat ball.

"No, I love it. I earn money, get fed by my customers and have all the tickles behind the ear a guy could want. But you know me, I love a whodunnit. Since you moved to town there has been a lot more action for us true crime fans," he smiled. Well at least someone was enjoying it all.

Quin babbled on about a show he had watched that had professional organizers come into a chaotic home and put everything in the right place. This seemed to be a round-a-bout way for him to get to his main point; the café office was a mess and he wanted me to give everything a makeover using designer baskets and acrylic storage bins. He kept using the word 'like' a lot and reassured me everything would be 'like, totally awesome.'

After explaining to him that he was the one making the mess, he seemed less interested in changing the system. He dumped purchase orders or receipts in the center of the floor and then I would come in and file them away for the accountant. Ideally Quin would sort some of it out himself, but he had shown no interest in the administrative side of running a business and I doubted it would change any time soon.

By the time we arrived at the hospital he had fallen asleep. The gentle rocking motion of the car over tarmac had lulled him into a nap and, as he couldn't come into the hospital with me, I wasn't going to wake him. I carefully opened the car door, grabbed my cell phone and slunk out onto the parking lot. I cracked the window an inch and parked in the shade of a large tree. It wasn't exactly hot today so I wasn't worried about him getting too warm.

I headed straight for the reception desk and explained that I had been called about Ms. Wright. I was taken to her room immediately and, despite the short walk to get there, my heart was racing with every step. The fact that no one had taken me aside to deliver bad news felt promising though.

"Oh good, you're awake," the nurse said as she pushed open the door and saw that Molly was sitting up in bed. I let out a weird squeaking noise as relief hit me and Molly laughed. "I'll go and find the doctor." The nurse left and I approached the chair beside the hospital bed, sitting down and feeling my heart rate stabilize.

"What happened?" I asked.

"I swerved to avoid hitting a squirrel," she laughed. "I guess the little guy decided to go for a late night stroll and I didn't see the ditch, once the front right wheel dipped over the edge there was nothing I could do. The car went in and the airbag went off, the only reason I'm here is because another driver called an ambulance for me. They must have seen the whole thing."

"A squirrel?" I repeated, skeptical at best.

"Yeah, I realize that squirrels can move pretty fast and I probably wouldn't have even hit it if I'd carried on driving straight," she smiled. "But I couldn't have something like that on my conscience."

"Are you injured? The nurse made it seem like you'd been unconscious."

"I'm beginning to ache, but it's nothing serious. I've had a few scans and everything looks fine. This happened hours ago and I just fell asleep here that's all. They must have tried that number a few times and then caught you when you broke into my house." I grimaced. I was sort of hoping there would be a way to keep my breaking-and-entering a secret, but Molly obviously knew that I had answered her home phone.

"I was worried. Rebecca said—"

"Oh Rebecca! I messaged her last night to say I would be coming back early and would open up the café with her, is she there on her own?" Molly said, straightening up suddenly and wincing in discomfort.

"She's fine, she had someone else come in to help. I felt as though I had said something that made you bail out of the hotel and, I don't know…" I paused. "After what happened with Lee I thought maybe someone had come after you."

"Yeah, a squirrel! I appreciate the concern though, I truly do. So did you find anything good in my apartment?" she smirked. I couldn't help but smile back. An hour ago I thought I would be walking in to quite a different scene at the hospital, now Molly was teasing me about my snooping. It was a relief.

"Is Charlie your area manager?" I asked. The smile on her face fell away. "I looked on your computer and I saw that you and Lee were both talking about someone called 'C', that stands for Charlie, right?" I was interrupted by the arrival of the doctor, the nurse that had escorted me was standing behind her.

"Are you a relative?" the doctor asked. I suspected that now was not a great time to lie, it didn't seem as sinister to do it over the phone when I had been concerned for Molly's safety but lying while *in front* of Molly felt different. I shook my head and the nurse offered to take me to the waiting area while the doctor ran through some questions with her patient.

"I'll see you back in Sucré," I said as I left. There was no need to stick around, I had to get to the University anyway and I felt as though Molly wasn't quite ready to give me the whole truth.

"Feel free to go back to my place," Molly yelled as I walked away. I looked back over my shoulder and she was smiling. She was letting me know that there was more for me to find there, she was giving me permission to be nosey. Maybe there was something that could lead me to the killer, maybe a more direct threat from Charlie or something.

By the time I got back to the car, Quin was stretching in his post-sleep groggy state, yawning with his mouth open as wide as it could get. "What took you so long?" he groaned. I checked the clock on the dashboard.

"I have barely been gone thirty minutes," I pointed out.

"Oh, well are you headed to that pet place or what?" he purred.

"No, I need to get to the lab. Do you want me to drop you off at home?" I asked.

"Where would you be snooping if you didn't need to go to work?"

"I'd probably go to Molly's house again and poke around her computer some more. Why?" I replied, sensing where this was heading.

"Drop me there, I can be an investigator too! I mean, you do it so it can't be that hard, right?" he meowed. I looked over and he was now somehow holding a large magnifying glass and his fuzzy cat nose was comically huge he held it up to his face and turned to me.

I had to consider that Quin might actually be helpful. I knew that I had to establish trust with him ahead of this assault course and with the mindset of 'fake it 'til you make it', I decided to go with his idea.

"Sure," I smiled. Quin beamed at me with delight that I wasn't fighting him on the matter. He had lived with my Aunt Edith for so long, he had probably seen my mom plenty. He was invested in this case too, he wanted to help.

I drove us back towards Sucré, the radio blasting out some hair metal number from the eighties that provoked a passionate air guitar performance on the passenger seat, and all the while I thought about how big this criminal enterprise could be.

There was a national pyramid scheme that was tangled up with a casino, there had been a murder and a layer of secrecy over all of it. I was recruiting a cat to help me solve it all. That probably would have to be edited out of any police reports when we got to the truth.

I dropped Quin off outside the apartment building and had him repeat the apartment number back to me a few times so I knew that he would be breaking into the right place.

By the time I had made it to the University of Awa, it seemed that Jeremy had already identified the blue substance as particularly moldy grass clippings. He was thrilled to tell me all about the process of working out what the sample was, and as he babbled away about the machine that had given him the answer I was transfixed on the cup in his hand.

"Jeremy, what is that?" I asked, pointing at the plastic shaker.

"Oh, I got into Nutraspin last week and it's great! I mean, it tastes terrible but look at my hair! They actually want to speak to me about being a brand ambassador, I can't see any harm in having a small, part time job. You have rearranged your hours to take care of other things and you seem to be doing great!" he said.

Oh boy.

1 5

I can't claim that my presentation to Jeremy was my finest work. I showed him a video online about the dangers of pyramid schemes, then drew a diagram to show the business model of Nutraspin. Clearly stating that this was a multi-level marketing ploy to get people recruited with no intention of helping those people make any money for themselves.

I was trying to keep my tone level, but I couldn't help getting angry at the people that had started the whole thing. Jeremy nodded along and gasped at the appropriate moments.

"Just to be clear, you are suggesting that this milkshake isn't actually doing anything beneficial for my body?" he asked.

"Are you... Jeremy you are a scientist, use your head! Do you maybe think your skin and hair look better because you are drinking more liquids now that you've added milkshakes into your daily life? Or have you changed other parts of your routine too?" I asked, breathing in and out in a slow, controlled way so that I didn't lose my cool.

"Oh, I did also go for a diamond facial with my mom at the weekend. While she was visiting she recommended this shampoo that 'boosts the bounce'," he laughed. "Yeah, now that you mention it there's a chance that these shakes haven't done much. They taste like liquidized cardboard."

He offered to let me try a sip, but he had hardly sold the flavor. We both laughed at how he would make a terrible salesman with a pitch like that, and I watched as he tipped the drink down the drain. It seemed as though I might have saved one prospective recruit from financial ruin, so at least my afternoon was going better than my morning had.

I went briefly into my office to see if any students had left papers on my desk; just one. I had offered to help with resumes as the careers advisor was currently off sick. This was just aimed at the kids in my classes, so mostly they were applying for science internships or further study in the biology field. I picked up the sheets of paper that had been stapled together and made my way back out of the science block and across the courtyard that the other buildings framed.

My security badge swung low on my lanyard, partially obscured by the document I was clutching to my chest. There was a moment of brief panic as the security guard, a giant uniformed bear named Lyle, stepped into my path to demand ID. I looked up at him with fear in my eyes as I scrambled for the laminated badge.

"Oh, Nora!" he chuckled. "Ah, yeah. Sorry. There has been a new 'ID everyone every time' policy, some final years played a prank on me last week and now I have to make sure people aren't switching badges around. I didn't mean to scare you."

"You're just doing your job, I understand," I replied. A bear standing on its hind legs is intimidating, even if you have known that bear for months. As a security guard he obviously was the perfect choice, it surprised me that any students had felt brave enough to mess with him.

"How's Quin? And that boyfriend of yours? I don't see a ring on that finger!" he teased. Lyle was a gossip, well maybe not with everyone, but definitely with me. He and Quin would often chat together and I suspected that some of Quin's less desirable traits had rubbed off on him.

"Oh, well...I...," I stammered. I was flustered like I had been ambushed by nosy relatives at thanksgiving, desperate to know the status of my love life and when there would be a wedding. In my defense, I had been married once already, hounding me for a second husband was just greedy. I had seen a vision of a wedding between Ryan and I, but there was no timeline for it. I supposed that just knowing it was somewhere on the horizon was enough.

"I'm just kidding," Lyle laughed. His bellow made his whole body shake and I nervously smiled and walked away. I already knew that his quip about our non-existent engagement was going to play on my mind for the rest of the day, I wish I had the ability to push those thoughts aside so that I could focus.

I got back to the car and locked myself inside, a habit I was trying to develop out of fear that the mafia would jump into the backseat while I was sat in the parking lot. I figured that they wouldn't be able to get me if the car door was locked, as if that would stop them. I'd seen gangster films before, I knew they could just break my car window or show up at my house. I guess I was giving myself a false sense of safety, but it was better than nothing.

I checked my cell phone and I didn't have any missed calls. I typed in Molly's home phone number and waited for Quin to pick up.

"Hello? You have reached that lady from the café," Quin answered.

"Quin, you know her name is Molly! Why would she answer her own phone like that?" I asked. The silence on the other end made me think he had silently shrugged his shoulders and was waiting for me to continue speaking. "Have you found anything?"

"Well she hasn't got a lot of fresh vegetables in the house, I found a couple of potatoes with roots growing out of them. It would be roots, right? The weird looking finger things that show up when you've let your potatoes get all nasty," he rambled.

"Okay, so she hasn't been to a grocery store lately. That's… that's really helpful, thank you," I said. I was forcing a sincere tone, but he seemed to be buying it.

"You're more than welcome. She also had a bunch of emails printed out and I double checked them on her computer and she had deleted them from her inbox, makes me think she was trying to establish a trail of evidence without their being a digital element that someone could hack into," he added.

"Wow, Quin! That's amazing! What were the emails about?" I asked.

"There were between her and someone signing off as 'C'," he said. I waited for more. "That's all I've got."

"What did 'C' say? What did Molly say?" I pushed.

"I can't remember."

"I'll be on my way soon, can't you read one out?" I pressed, impatient for information.

"Ah, yeah. That's going to be a challenge captain," he sighed.

"Why?" I replied, dryly.

"I recycled them all. I mean, they said at the bottom that they shouldn't be printed out unless absolutely necessary. In the interest of the planet and our ever-changing climate you should try to go digital as much as possible, am I right? So I threw them all in the paper bin and took it out for the recycling truck. I can hear them coming up the street now," he said. I started the engine.

I understood that, at this point, there was nothing Quin could do. He could hardly go outside and drag the paper bin back into the house in case anyone saw him. I was surprised he managed to get it out to the curb without being seen.

"I will be there soon, don't touch anything," I said. I hung up knowing full well that Quin was likely about to do something even less helpful than his destruction of evidence. I pulled away from the parking lot and began hurtling along the road towards Sucré. Those trucks move slowly, right? Maybe I could get there in time to stop Molly's recycling being taken away.

Ryan called as I was driving and I answered through the speakerphone. "Hey, how is your day going?" he asked.

"You don't want to know, I mean that sincerely," I replied. "How are you?"

"I'm all right. I've spoken with your mom and the police at the station. I think that they are looking to make a formal arrest based off Herb's witness testimony," he explained. I felt my heart sink.

"Ah. Not good," I managed. "Have you seen Herb's timeline? What has he said?"

"What we already know, nothing different. He saw your mom in the store and she was yelling at Lee. He stepped away to give them some privacy and then the next thing you know, Lee is dead and your mom is gone. His cameras are just for show, he doesn't have them plugged in and hasn't since 2009 apparently. His statement is making this difficult to fight. If Molly or Rebecca could give a detailed time-line of your mom's whereabouts…"

"Well Molly is in hospital and Rebecca is at the café. Rebecca would be the easier choice there," I explained.

"Hospital? What happened?" he gasped.

"Swerved to avoid a squirrel and wrecked her own car," I said. "I've been over to see her and she's awake and chatty. Rebecca would still be easiest to get hold of though."

"Jeez, lucky squirrel. I can go and speak to Rebecca then. What are you doing now?" he asked.

"I left Quin at Molly's place and he has just thrown a bunch of potential evidence into a recycling bin and left it curbside for pickup, so I have to intervene," I laughed. "If I think about it too much then I could cry, so I am trying to focus on the funny side."

"Good luck with that," he chuckled. "I'll have to go, someone has just brought another box of Nutraspin documents for us to look through. It's very much 'death by a thousand papercuts' in here today. I love you, see you later."

He hung up before I said it back, but I was outside Molly's house now. I could see the recycling truck up the street and grabbed the paper bin quickly, unlocked the door to the building and ran up the stairs to the apartment.

"Yeah… you were too late," Quin groaned. I opened the plastic box and realized it was heavy due to a few wet newspapers in the bottom that had become stuck to the box and hadn't fallen out when the recy-cling truck people tipped it upside down. *Darn it.*

"Well it's not over until it's over," Quin said, sitting a little taller and giving the look that I knew meant trouble wasn't far away.

"What are you about to suggest?"

"The reason I have gotten all those warning letters is because I got caught, but if you are in on it too then we would be able to investigate in a different way," he grinned. "I think we just show up outside the recycling plant and walk in, we can be invisible or something."

"I've done the 'invisibility' thing before, well *Ryan* did it. I don't know exactly how he did it, Quin, and it seemed like a lot of work. Is this just an excuse for you to snoop about in the garbage again?"

"Yeah, probably because that boyfriend of yours was wasting time setting up the wishing well method. I have a better way… elasticated body suit!"

"What?" I sighed.

"Hear me out. I can whip us up a pair of form fitting cat suits with gloves and a big hood, it acts *just* like an invisibility cloak but without the worry that it would fall off if you started running. I'm actually thinking of selling them online!"

"Sure," I conceded. I leaned against the counter and watched as Quin set to work on his own bizarre brand of familiar magic to create the body suits in our sizes. He had been so convinced that the garbage trucks in Sucré were involved in money laundering, but now I thought that Nutraspin and the casino were *also* laundering money. Could they all be connected? We were about to find out.

16

_D_o you ever have those moments when you catch your reflection while you are in the middle of doing something stupid and just think, 'what bad choices have I made in my life to end up here'? That was what happened to me on the way to the garbage and recycling plant, only I couldn't see my own reflection on account of wearing an invisibility jumpsuit with built-in gloves and a face mask that my cat had designed.

I could no longer see Quin, obviously, and he told me that we shouldn't speak in case we drew attention to ourselves and get busted by another witch in town. It was quite likely that one or two of the magical folk in Sucré would be able to sense us nearby, but as long as we tried to stay out of people's way then we should get to our destination uninterrupted.

I regretted not driving a little closer to the recycling plant and then getting changed in the car, but we couldn't have a vehicle gliding around town without a visible driver, people would freak out. The material for the jumpsuit was unusual; cold to the touch and it would slip off my hands like it was made of water or oil.

I had half expected it to feel cold when I had worn it, but my body temperature was rapidly climbing and I desperately wanted to feel the breeze on my skin. The catastrophizer in me was convinced that I would overheat, pass out, and remain lying on the sidewalk for eternity as no one would ever find me. I realized that was a very dramatic thought to entertain, but I couldn't help it. I had no idea where Quin had gotten to, so I had to assume he was still walking in the right direction.

As far as I knew, his investigation into the garbage men of Sucré had only gone as far as him diving into the back of their truck, he hadn't made it all the way back to their base before. This left me doubting that he actually knew the address, but I had driven past the place once or twice so was getting close. The smell in the air confirmed it.

How would I know if Quin had made it? I walked towards the open gate of the yard that one of the garbage trucks had driven through and found myself standing at the edge of an enormous facility. Sucré had implemented quite an advanced recycling program and it was being used as a successful model for other towns to mirror. Quin would have you believe that they expanded the facility in order to move money around more easily.

The trucks were all operated by one company that was contracted by the town council. They made rounds of Sucré several times a week to make sure all community trash cans were emptied regularly and would make requested stops outside businesses to help keep alley ways clear of garbage.

Obviously this sounds great, but this would also be a great cover story if you were in fact committing crimes and needed to subtly increase the amount of vehicles on the streets without arousing suspicion. I'm sure I didn't used to be so skeptical; I think Quin dragged me down to his level. Annoyingly though, he isn't always wrong.

The gate mechanism began to whirr behind me and I realized I was about to be trapped here. I couldn't just use my magic to escape incase Quin was in here too, then he would be trapped here alone. I wasn't worried about him, I was worried about how much damage he could do if he was left unsupervised for too long.

I backed up to the fence to make sure that no one bumped into me by mistake. This was a busy area and there were trucks driving in all directions as they deposited the garbage into the correct areas and then parked up. I saw the recycling truck that had been on Molly's street, I recognized the license plate. The guys jumped out of the cab and one of them pushed the button to open the sides of the truck.

I couldn't believe what I was seeing, but I had to hope that Quin was seeing it too.

The truck was built specifically to collect different types of recyclable goods, with slots on the side that allowed the guys collecting it to deposit glass, plastic, paper etc.... into the right place. There appeared to be several hidden compartments that were revealed by manually unlocking them. This was exactly what Quin had tried to warn me about.

I watched as one guy lifted out three separate duffel bags and carried them into the office building. Another grabbed a box of paper recycling that he had separated from the rest. Was this the stuff from Molly's apartment? I heard a sniffing noise at my feet, after a flicker of panic that I had been discovered by a guard dog, I realized it was Quin.

"Well, I bet you feel pretty silly now," he purred. He had been right about this, or at least it was looking like he had been right, so he would be insufferable for months. "Do you want to dive through the garbage first? Or go into the office to see what those sketchy looking guys are doing?"

"I felt silly the moment I agreed to let you make me an outfit," I teased. "But I think that following the bad guys is the way to go. Feel free to roll about in trash if that would make you happy." I heard the very gentle sound of his feet patting on the ground as he ran towards the large compost heap. Aren't cats famed for being tidy, clean creatures? I think Quin must have a defect.

I saw bits of fruit peel and a half-eaten fish fly up into the air as he landed on top of it all. I made a mental note to stay at Ryan's place tonight, Quin was going to smell awful for a long time. I jogged towards the office entrance, dodging a truck that was rolling slowly across the center of the area, and slipped through the automatic doors behind one of the guys carrying a duffle bag.

They walked into a conference room and there was a woman at the head of the table, carefully painting one of her fingernails and not acknowledging anybody that walked in. They placed the bags down on the table in front of her and unzipped them. It was cash. Not just small amounts, but huge chunks of cash, just like the rolls we had found in Lee's storage unit.

I saw the guy begin to tip out the papers onto the desk and I panicked. If this was all related to Nutraspin laundering money, and Molly was caught printing out emails that could link these people back to the crimes, then she could be in immeasurable danger.

I whispered, 'Verto', aiming my hands at the box. I was tucked deep into the far corner of the room to avoid anyone walking into me and I hoped that no one heard me using magic. I had used a spell to swap the contents. I had also focused on summoning, a spell that I had been practicing silently so that I could use it in situations like this. Well, not *exactly* like this, who could have predicted how my day would go when I woke up this morning?

"What is this?" the woman said. She picked up the closest sheet of paper.

"Printed out emails. It looks like Wright was trying to get out, looks like the beginning of blackmail to me," one of the men explained.

"This is a printout of a Thai restaurant menu, as is this one, and this one," she said, lifting up sheet after sheet. I had done the right thing; I had swapped out the papers just in time to keep Molly safe for a while longer.

"Molly won't leave, I know she won't," the woman scoffed. "She might have grand ideas about exposing us but I don't think she is brave enough to act out against family."

She had to be talking about Charlie, suggesting that Molly wouldn't get her brother in trouble. Maybe this woman was right, but if Molly had considered it, then it must mean she wanted an escape route to get away from this situation.

"I heard she's in the hospital, so at least we don't need to worry about her for a few days. I wonder if she's faking it as an excuse to ignore my messages," the woman mused.

"I hate to be the barer of bad news, but it looks like the FDA is looking to make another visit," someone else said. This cause the woman to pound the table in anger. I flinched.

"Just make sure it's clean everywhere that they might go. I need to speak to Charlie," she huffed, disappearing through the door in a whirlwind. The others followed close behind and took the bags of money with them, leaving behind the takeout menu print-outs and the nail polish.

I stepped closer to see if there was anything else to take from that conversation, maybe someone had left a notepad or something. I reached out and grabbed the nail polish, slipped it into the pocket that Quin had sewn into the thigh of the body suit, and snuck out of the door without being seen.

Two men were talking in the corridor as I crept past.

"It's a ten thousand dollar buy in apparently, it might be fun to watch," one of them said.

"Jeez," the other one replied, whistling at the sound of all that money. "Maybe I should get into the poker circuit," he laughed.

Poker? Was this whole Nutraspin thing just a cover to help launder money from illegal gambling? My head was starting to ache, I don't remember when I had last drank anything and I was trying to unravel five million mysteries at once. The woman had said 'Charlie', so it must be related to the casino. Lee had all that cash with him, he must have been helping to move the money around, as well as all the garbage men. Was Molly laundering money for them too?

I sloped away from the conversation after they had confirmed the address of the poker match aloud, then snuck outside through the doors as they opened to let someone in. The slight movement on top of the compost heap signified that Quin was still playing in the dirt.

"Quin," I whispered when I got close enough. "We should go." I heard a sigh of disappointment as he shuffled off towards the ground beside me.

My cell phone began to ring loudly in my pocket and all the people that were working nearby began to look around in a panic, realizing that there might be someone on the inside of the fence that shouldn't be there. The gate rolled aside as another truck pulled up and we sprinted to get out before we were caught. My phone eventually stopped ringing as we were halfway up the sidewalk and we dipped into an alleyway to remove the bodysuits that were hiding us from the world.

"What now?" Quin asked.

"I think I need to speak to the police," I began. No one is moving cash like this if it's legal, if the cops hadn't found all the money in Lee's storage unit then they soon would. I needed to push them to hurry up. I asked Quin to make his way back to the Catmosphere Café and told him that I would head to the station to speak to Brent. Maybe he could help me explain away the magic involved in the evidence I had collected so far.

Quin didn't think it was a good idea, but I was running out of time before they formally arrested my mom. He sprinted off up the high street and I stepped out into the sunlight to begin walking, but Ryan was running in my direction and yelling.

What now?

17

"There you are," he panted. Where had he been running from? "Where's the fire?" I joked.

"I tried to call you but you didn't answer, I just spoke with Rebecca and it seems like the timeline doesn't match up for your mom to have been the one to kill Lee. She said your mom went to the bathroom at one point, but there is no exit onto the street or anything. Your mom wasn't in the flower shop at all," Ryan explained.

We had been walking together since he joined me, but now I stopped. I could see the police station from where I was standing. Ryan followed my eye-line to see what I had been looking at, then turned back to me.

"What were you about to do?" he asked.

"I was going to speak to Brent about the fact that I've just seen some woman at the garbage facility being handed bags of cash. People there were talking about some underground poker night. It's illegal gambling and that woman mentioned Charlie's name. I think they should be looking into the casino," I said, realizing as I heard my own words that maybe I didn't have enough to go on.

"Your mom wasn't at the flower shop, that is the thing to focus on first. The issue now is that Herb said he saw her there, so either he is lying, or Rebecca is. I suppose we took it as a given that your mom was actually there, I obviously dropped the ball by not double checking sooner," he sighed.

"So did I," I said, fighting back a smile. It obviously wasn't funny, but for us both to have overlooked such a significant part of the case was maddening. I can be a scatter brain for sure, Ryan is usually better at these things. He must be distracted by something, probably just worrying about how I am coping with all this. Ryan's mouth was turning upwards in the corners, he clearly was seeing the funny side too.

"Okay, so we should go back to Herb and check in with him. If we can clear this all up then we can take *this* information to the police. I think we have to prioritize clearing your mom's name with regards to murder, only after that has happened should we be describing other crimes to the cops."

He was right. I had to assume that investigating money laundering would take a long time. Once my mom was free then they could spend all their time looking into that, but for now I needed them to let her out. We walked towards the flower shop and a little bell rang to announce our arrival.

The interior décor had changed significantly since my last visit. All of the displays had moved around, windchimes hung from every available space and the floor tiles had been deep cleaned. It was impossible for us to get much closer to the desk without knocking into hanging metal and bamboo that played a whimsical tune. Herb appeared from a back room; he had something behind his back.

"Oh, it's you," he sighed. I watched relief wash over his pale face and a shaking hand emerge from behind him to place a shiny handgun on the counter. Why was he armed? The tension in his shoulders was still there and I sensed that he was still expecting something bad to happen.

"Herb, what's with the gun?" I asked. He gulped. "Is this because of what happened to Lee?"

"I... I shouldn't..." he stammered.

"You weren't honest with the police were you, that's why you're afraid," Ryan began. "You lied to Nora and to the officers that attended the crime scene, you were told to lie by the real killer. Am I close?"

Herb ran around the counter and over to the front door, locking us in with him. He spoke now in a whisper as if he thought he might be overheard by people on the street.

"I don't know what I can say," he said. "I know I did the wrong thing, but…"

"Someone threatened you," Ryan interrupted, the nod from Herb suggested that he was correct. "That's why you've added all these windchimes, so you know when somebody comes in and you can arm yourself."

"It was a stranger. They came in and the man looked terrified, he started to grovel, and I was ordered to give them some privacy. I didn't want any trouble so I walked away. By the time I came back out, your stepdad was dead. She told me to say that the guys wife came in, she showed me a picture of her so I could point her out," Herb sobbed. The tears were flowing silently down his cheeks, but his breathing was unsteady.

A woman had killed Lee and threatened the witness, made him blame my mom for it.

"Would you recognize the woman if you saw her again? Could you describe her?" I asked. My understanding of the criminal organization we were investigating was minimal, I had seen Molly's brother, a bunch of garbage men and one mystery woman. Could it be her?

"What if she comes back?" he shuddered.

"She won't," Ryan assured him. I saw the glint in Ryan's eye and took it to mean that he would put some sort of protection spell over the place to keep Herb safe from the repercussions of his amended witness statement. Something about Ryan's tone seemed to convince Herb enough to speak.

"She had brown hair; it had a few streaks of caramel as if the sun had bleached it in places. An expensive looking necklace with matching earrings. She had sharp features, a nose that came to a point and chiseled cheek bones, bright red lipstick. I think her nails were red too," he explained.

His description might not be enough for the police to sketch out the suspect, but it was enough for me. I reached into my pocket and pulled the nail polish out, gesturing towards Ryan so that he could see the red colored bottle. It must have been her.

I had been in the room with the killer and hadn't known it. Who was she? Why would she have killed Lee? Had he found out too much about her illegal activities? With so many unknowns, I could understand why Herb had a gun.

"Look, let's go and straighten things out with the police. I can make sure you are safe and hopefully we can get Ms. Jackson out of jail," Ryan said, smiling at both Herb and I. Herb seemed reluctant, but ultimately agreed to do so. I had to assume Ryan was using every ounce of charm to convince Herb to go with him, he was easy to trust and his determination to get the truth out was motivating me to keep going, despite the obstacles we still faced.

I had yet to return to Molly's apartment, even though she had suggested there were clues there that could give me answers. Ryan and Herb continued to discuss their next moves, and I interrupted briefly to tell Ryan where I was going.

Would there be any way to identify the woman in question by looking through Molly's things? Maybe Molly knew her somehow, or this person had posted in the Nutraspin forum. I let myself out of the flower shop and navigated through the streets back to the apartment building.

It was late afternoon and I had been running on adrenaline for most of the day. The ache in my muscles was catching up with me and I tried to remember the last time I had sat down to relax. It felt as though I had to keep going until my mom was free, like me getting a few hours of sleep would be a waste of my time.

Inside Molly's apartment, everything was the same as we had left it. I could see where Quin had gone through the papers, wait... the emails! I had swapped them out at the office so that the scary woman couldn't read them, but they must have gone somewhere. I began to open cupboards and drawers, hoping that somehow, I had sent them back here.

I opened a ring binder that was tucked down the side of the desk, reading a message that Molly had sent to 'C'. I had them. I slumped onto the sofa and poured myself into the printouts in my hands. Some of the messages were friendly; innocuous correspondence between two professionals. They discussed Nutraspin sales, other ways in which Molly could market the product to local people and ways in which she could expand her business through social media.

Other messages were thick with hostility. Molly had suggested that she had only promised to try this sales position for a few months, and that those months had passed. She hadn't seen a boost to her income, in fact it was costing her more money than she was making, so she was suggesting it was time for her to step away. 'C' made it clear that leaving wasn't an option.

I found one message that seemed to be between two entirely different people. It was still the same email addresses for both Molly and 'C', but they were discussing a family brunch, which wines they should bring and the thickness of jackets that they both thought would be best for the weather that weekend. It was like two old friends were speaking, or family members. This had to be Charlie.

The phone began to ring on the kitchen counter, and I jumped up to answer it. It was Molly.

"Nora?" she said as I picked up.

"Yeah, just snooping around your house again," I laughed. "Being nosy is just as much fun as you'd think it is."

"Found anything good yet?" she asked.

"I'm not sure, I found some email print outs between you and your brother, but that's about it," I said.

"My brother? Charlie never emails me," she replied in a confused tone. "I printed out emails from the regional manager for Nutraspin, are those the ones you are looking at?"

"Oh… I thought the 'C' at the bottom was your brother just using his initials," I explained.

"No, I told you. Charlie isn't all that bad, he just… he has made some questionable choices, let's put it that way," she laughed.

"Do you know a woman involved in Nutraspin? Dark hair, red

nails—" I had barely described the mystery female before Molly let out a loud burst-laugh in surprise.

"That's Charlie's wife, Francesca. We all call her 'Chessie' for short, at her insistence," she scoffed. "She is the one that got me into Nutraspin, she is the 'C' at the bottom of those emails." I held the phone closer to my ear as I waited to hear more, but Molly simply stopped talking. Did she know what that woman had done?

"How much do you know about Chessie?" I asked.

"I know that she has plenty of money already, so it makes no sense for her to be trying to sell wellness shakes as a side hustle. Have you seen the car she drives? I don't understand their finances, but Charlie said they are both doing very well for themselves. They had been talking and talking about their retirement plans, their dreams of travelling the world while they were young enough to enjoy it.

"It was after I spoke to them that I got into the idea of retiring early, so Chessie helped me sign up as a Nutraspin representative. I quickly realized that it wasn't headed anywhere positive for me and wanted to leave, she was quite insistent that I give it more time," she explained. I already knew that, I'd seen the emails.

Molly's sister-in-law was the murderer, right? Herb had seen her in the flower shop yelling at Lee, then threatened Herb to keep his mouth shut about what he knew. She was clearly getting her money illegally and she had plans to host a poker game tonight to get even more cash. I had to hope Ryan knew how to play, because in a few short hours we would be at an underground gambling event surrounded by criminals.

I'd need all the luck I could get.

18

"Let me get this straight," Ryan began. "You want us to walk right into the belly of the beast and infiltrate an illegal poker game because... I feel like I'm missing something." I had sent Ryan a text message asking him to join me in Molly's apartment. While I had been waiting for him, I had pulled one photo album after another down from shelves and confirmed that Molly and the mystery woman knew each other.

So many of them were labelled 'Charlie and Chessie on beach day', or 'Chessie in her Christmas sweater'. The version of Chessie that I had seen at the garbage facility had been polished, perfectly put together and elegant, with just a twist of an intimidating snarl. Chessie in the photographs had on old clothes, was smiling with her whole face and looked happy. Something had obviously changed.

Among the pictures was one that had been cut out of a newspaper that had written a feature of Chessie and her award from the community. She had been recognized for her work in the recycling department and they had surprised her with a trophy and a bunch of flowers. She looked embarrassed in the photograph, trying to mask her overalls and boots.

I showed the pictures to Ryan so he would know who we were

looking for. He was still pacing around the living room as I sat on the sofa waiting for him to speak again. I understood that he wanted to avoid putting us in a dangerous position, but I didn't know when we would have the opportunity to get all the bad guys in one room again.

"Ryan, I just think that if we could get some sneaky footage of them all gathered at the poker table, make sure Chessie's face is on camera, then we could hand over that evidence to the police. Otherwise I have nothing to give them other than Herb's description of a brunette. I can hardly say, 'I made myself invisible and snuck into the office to watch crimes happen,'" I explained.

"Fair enough," he smiled. He came to sit beside me and took both of my hands in his. "I just feel like you are more willing to take risks because of what's at stake. I want to get your mom out too, but we have to be sensible about this."

"I am," I assured him. "This isn't some wild idea that has come out of nowhere, I've seen it in at least three films." That made him laugh a little and I felt as though I had convinced him.

"If Charlie is there then he will recognize both of us. We should disguise ourselves," he said. With a snap of his fingers a game of Guess Who appeared on the coffee table in front of us and we both turned to face the board. At this point I didn't need to say the words aloud anymore, just think them.

The face I have is just for me, I now will change what others see, take my canvas, wash it clean, to paint upon what shall be seen, when I decide to change it back, I give my face a painful smack.'

I flipped down the faces that didn't meet up with my vision of myself for the poker game, knocking over women with incredibly long blonde hair, women with nose rings, and a women with brown eyes and an amber streak across one of them that looked suspiciously similar to my usual self.

I wandered away from the sofa to check myself out in the nearest mirror, the fizzing sensation across my skin had happened suddenly, much quicker than it had in the past, and so I knew my appearance must have changed.

I found a bathroom mirror and looked at my new face and was

impressed with the result. My hair was a vibrant orange and pinned up elegantly with curls tumbling loose around my ears. I had diamond earrings that sparkled in the light and matched the silver headband that was slotted into my updo. A beautiful gown made from a turquoise silk gave me a formal look, the train was stretched across the ground.

I suspected that the type of gambling event I was going to wasn't going to involve such fancy attire, so I tapped at the dress just above my knee and the fabric below that point fell away, the silk shifting into an expensive looking cotton of the same color. Now I looked like I worked in an office as an executive or something.

I walked back out of the bathroom and was met by Ryan as a new man. He was in a pinstripe suit and his greying curls had been replaced by short, dark hair. He looked broader across the shoulders and had an unapproachable air to him that he hadn't had before.

"Shall we?" he asked, offering his arm. I wrapped my manicured hands around him and concentrated on the address that the men at the garbage facility had let slip. I obviously didn't want to transport us right into the venue of the event, so had us appear in an alley a street or two over.

Until the voice rang out behind us, I hadn't realized exactly where we were. But as Charlie emerged from a fire exit at the back of the casino, I saw that we were in the parking lot right behind 'Sky Roller'.

"Hey, you guys shouldn't be here," Charlie said. I whipped my head round to offer an apology, but as soon as our eyes locked, I knew that we were busted. "Nora?"

"No, who is Nora?" I said, shakily. "My name is Christine, and I—"

"No, you are Nora Wildes," he insisted. He quickly closed the gap between us with three large strides and I saw Ryan's hand twitch as he considered using his magic to defend us. "I know. I *know*, you know?"

"What?" I replied.

"Look, I may not be a full witch myself, but I have dabbled in the realms of magic before. I can sense who you are, I knew when you came into the casino and I know it now."

"You have magic?" Ryan asked.

"Just a bit. Molly said you guys might be back," he sighed. I gulped, fearful that Molly had never been on our side and had sent us into the lion's den. How could telling him that we were coming be helpful to us? I felt like we had been ambushed.

"Oh," I managed.

"No, it's not... I know that you guys are trying to make all this craziness end, and I want to help you," he whispered. "Chessie has become someone that I barely recognize. She started acting differently, taking unnecessary risks and then getting really aggressive any time I questioned her. She has paid off all of my security in the casino to defend *her* business interests above mine, so I had to speak to you guys like that the other day because she had people in the room that might have reported back."

"I don't understand, so you're not involved?" Ryan asked.

"No. We met years ago, fell in love and got married. Everything was going so well, but she got suckered in to Nutraspin and that was the beginning of the downfall. All the other women she would meet were so glamourous and no matter how good she looked; it was never enough. She wanted more, more spa days, more hair salon appointments... she thought if she looked like some reality star that people would buy more of those stupid shakes."

"Did it work?" I said.

"For a while, but greed is a powerful drug. We couldn't afford for her to live this way, even with her Nutraspin income and the takings from the casino. She started looking up all these wild ideas online, then she came up with the poker night. Poached a few of my biggest customers and invited them to an exclusive event. It worked, word spread to the whole town and then she started getting people that wanted to gamble with even larger amounts," he said, letting out a sigh.

"But they weren't getting their money legally," Ryan guessed.

"I don't know, honestly. It's very much a 'don't ask questions' type night. Rich people playing with money like it's nothing, Chessie takes a cut as the host and then she has been filtering it through Nutraspin. I know she has been trying to push it through my casino too, but I've made my feelings about it clear. She scares me, I don't know what she is capable of."

Charlie was glistening with nervous sweat and it made me think that he had truly no idea that she might have killed someone. I wanted to burst out the truth, tell him everything that Herb had said and that I had seen her handling all that money back at the garbage facility. He already knew about the cash though.

"Charlie, I don't know how to say this. I think your wife killed my step-father," I announced.

"In Sucré? She has been over there a lot over the past week," he sighed. "I had suspected it when I found out his name in the paper. I recognized it from one of her spreadsheets. It didn't seem like a coincidence, but I had no proof."

He looked a little shaken up, but also relieved, as if it was a good feeling to have your worst thought validated. He thought his wife had become a master criminal capable of anything, and he was right. His hands were fidgeting more now though, and he was shifting between one foot and the other. It was a lot to handle.

"Would she confess? If you cornered her about it?" Ryan asked.

"I don't think she has said a word of truth to me in months, but I suppose I could try. If she sets her men on me then I can't defend myself, I can only do basic spells. I don't know how..." he stammered.

"We will protect you. If we can get her on record confessing to the murder, or even just catch her admitting her involvement in all of the money laundering then it would get the police to take action with an investigation. Right?" I said, looking more to Ryan than Charlie.

Ryan gave me a nod. Charlie reluctantly nodded too. He led the way and Ryan held my hand tighter as we approached the venue. The next thirty minutes could be make or break for getting my mom off the hook. My intuition was making my stomach rumble and I feared that things were about to get messier.

"A kiss for luck?" Ryan smiled. We would need all the luck we could get.

19

There was a basement entrance from the street, taking us into a dark, cloudy room beneath a restaurant. Cigar smoke and the scent of luxury cologne was thick and made me cough, but I tried hard to suppress the reflex so as not to draw attention to myself.

There was a table in the center and shelving lining each wall. It was strange to see all these folks trying to act so high and mighty when they were surrounded by canned beans and bags of pasta. There was a solitary waitress handing out drinks from a tray to the gamblers that were waiting in their seats for the game to begin. Chessie was visibly counting money at a desk in the corner.

Charlie stayed stood behind us so that Chessie didn't spot him. Although no one was really looking at us. I figured that they might ask for ID or something, after all we were a couple of unknowns walking in off the street watching them engage in illegal activity. Surely there would be more security.

"They can see us, but they won't pay much attention. A little spell of mine," Charlie whispered. *Perfect.* Even if they did notice us, no one would recognize our faces. Chessie stepped back to the table and handed out the chips with the assistance of the waitress who had now set the drinks tray down.

"As you know, it was a $2k buy in. Jason will be your dealer tonight and bets are limitless, we keep going until we drop or you're all broke," she joked. There was a scattered laugh, followed by silence as they began to examine the cards that Jason had dealt.

"What are we looking for?" I whispered. I peered over to see that Ryan was recording on his smart phone through a small hole in the top pocket of his blazer.

"Well she is definitely involved in this," he replied. "I guess we just film what we can and then sneak out. I don't really have a plan." He smiled at me with his altered face and I smiled back. What were we hoping she would do? Immediately announce her involvement in a murder to this room full of people, or maybe tell them all what she does with the cash once they've left?

"Are you sure you don't want to play tonight?" one of the men asked Chessie. He was giving her a flirtatious look and she reciprocated. "Come on, it would be fun. You could pull up a chair right next to me."

She stepped closer to whisper something in his ear and I could sense Charlie tensing up. We weren't the only spectators. There were at least a dozen other people at the edges of the room sipping drinks and watching the game intently. I had to wonder if this often led to cheating.

I had seen plenty of films where people had set up some sort of secret language for communicating as to whether the other players had good cards or not. Maybe the spectating partner would cough or order another champagne every time someone was bluffing. I had to assume that the people watching knew that this was all illegal.

I stared at them each in turn, trying to see if signals were being sent to the players at the table. "What did she whisper?" Charlie hissed in my ear. "What did she say?"

"I don't know," I replied in a hushed voice. There was no music to add to the ambience, just the sound of cigarette lighters clicking and the occasional snap of fingers to get the waitresses attention. I could hear my pulse in my ears, pounding loudly as the players each debated their next moves.

Chessie wiggled over to the man that had spoken to her earlier and whispered something else. The man laughed. Charlie was fuming at this, as if the fact that his wife was a criminal and potentially also a murderer wasn't enough to deter his affections.

"Hey Chess, is it true you smoked a guy over in Sucré?" another man asked. She looked up at him through narrowed eyes and her lips tightened before breaking into a sickening grin. "Man, I knew it. You take care of business, no one messes with you. What did the sucker do then, huh?"

The room snickered as they watched for her reply. She stood up straight, leaning away from the man she had been flirting with, and began to walk slowly around the table. It was like a victory lap and a peacock presentation rolled into one.

"You guys all know how I clean cash. It's well known that those types of things should stay private, am I right?" she grinned. "Some bozo decided to tell his wife all about it, then the two of them were conspiring to expose me to the cops. Now the guy is dead and the wife is in jail for it. She knows not to mess with me now."

Fury bubbled beneath the surface of my skin, how could she be bragging about this? I looked back to see how Charlie was handling the confession, but he was already pushing through the gap between Ryan and I and starting to yell.

"Maybe some people are in happy marriages, Chess. Maybe they trusted each other enough to have honest conversations about the mess they were in before it got too far, and you've broken them," he shrieked.

Chessie's demeanor wavered. She struggled to maintain the stern look as her husband actively sobbed in front of her and raised a judgmental finger at her to continue his shouting.

"Charl—"

"Don't Charlie me, I should have spoken up sooner but you have had me under your thumb for so long that I didn't even know that I could act out against you. When you signed up to that pyramid scheme I warned you that it was bad news, you ignored me. I showed you one article after another by journalists investigating that stupid wellness shake company and you went ahead with it anyway. I should have been more insistent, Chess. I should have…"

He was struggling to get the words out now, which seemed to give Chessie the boost she needed to try more bravado.

"My husband, ladies and gentlemen. I'm sure you've seen him before, he runs 'Sky Roller' and seems to have completely lost his spine," she scoffed.

"What are you gonna do to him?" the guy she had flirted with asked. I sensed that he was trying to goad her into hurting Charlie, using him as a sacrificial lamb to establish her dominance once again and make sure people understood that she didn't take threats lightly.

"Chessie, please. Let's just go to the cops, explain everything and get your conscience cleaned. Please. Do your time, step away from all of this and when you get out of jail in thirty years we can pick up where we left off," Charlie pleaded. I didn't think mentioning three decades of imprisonment was a great persuasion technique.

"That's not how these things work," she said, head high and her fingers laced in front of her. "You need to realize how great money is, especially if you have a lot of it, which I do. Sometimes if you want the finer things in life you have to take a few risks."

"And killing my step-father was a risk worth taking?" I blurted out. *Dang.* I had definitely drawn attention to myself that Charlie's spell wouldn't be able to protect me from. Ryan wrapped his arm around the back of me and grabbed at my waist, he was ready to sprint out of here if it got too dangerous and I assume I would have to transport us to a safe distance as soon as we were away from prying eyes.

A large man dressed in all black stepped in front of the door through which we had entered. "I know about people like you," Chessie announced. "I should have known you would use some freaky tricks to get back at me for killing that man."

"It's over, Francesca. Just accept defeat," Ryan interjected. The players at the poker table put their cards down and I saw a few of them reach into their jackets. If everyone in this room had brought a weapon then things were about to get messy. If Chessie was arrested then there was a risk that she might expose all of the people in here gambling, I doubted they would let that happen easily.

"I'd say you're outnumbered, wouldn't you," she scoffed. "You won't leave here alive."

At that threat, everyone stood up very suddenly. Guns drawn and aiming in all directions. As people started to look around, guns were re-aimed. The man that had flirted with Chessie had a gun aimed right at her. Of the eight people sat at the poker table, six of them had stood up to point at other gamblers in the room, as had the security guard at the door and a few of the spectators.

"What is this?" Chessie gasped. Her facade was slipping as she tried to comprehend what was happening. I was confused myself. One of the gamblers tried to take a step backwards and the man that had flirted with Chessie moved his arm to aim at him, at which point Chessie stepped forwards and slapped him hard across the face. That was when the real chaos began.

The skin of the man's face began to wobble and swirl, I recognized it immediately as the transformation that occurs at the end of a disguise spell. Whoever this person was had used the same magic as Ryan and I. Chessie looked horrified as the man morphed into somebody new. It was Officer Brent Murphy from the Sucré police department, my ex-boyfriend.

I gasped enough that Brent looked over, we locked eyes. I knew he had inherited magic from his dead Uncle and that he had been training with O.W.L. just like I was. It never occurred to me that he would be using magic to infiltrate a crime ring.

The other gun wielding officers revealed themselves, pulling police badges out of pockets followed by handcuffs. They weren't all from Sucré, Brent was the only officer I recognized. I wondered if anyone else was using disguise magic. No one apart from Chessie had seemed too concerned with the face shifting man in the room, so maybe they all knew about witches already.

One by one, the guilty people in the room were arrested and escorted out to waiting police vans. Charlie was also taken out in handcuffs as he had clearly known about all this for some time. Brent took Chessie up the basement steps and asked that we wait for him. Chessie protested loudly all the way back up to street level and was only silenced when the van doors closed behind her and she was driven away.

Ryan wrapped himself around me tightly and I melted into his arms. His heavy breathing let me know that he had thought he wasn't sure how this was going to go and was relieved that we were both uninjured. He leaned back and kissed me, using his magic to restore our appearances back to normal.

"There are ways other than 'getting slapped' to end that spell," he laughed.

"I wish someone had told me that," Brent joked as he returned to the basement. A red handprint glowing on his left cheek. "I should probably explain what just happened, I'm sure that was not what you expected."

I had a million questions and I knew Ryan must have some too. Did Brent know all along that my mom was innocent? Was her arrest just to make Chessie think she had gotten away with it? How long had they been tracking her? If they knew Chessie had done it, why not arrest her sooner?

Before I had the chance to speak, the heavy stomping sound of someone charging down the stairs distracted me. There was shouting from the street and when I saw what was happening, I could guess why. Charlie was standing in the basement, still handcuffed, with one of the police officer's guns. There were more footsteps, more noise. Police stormed the room with weapons drawn. It was a frenzy.

"This is for my wife!" he yelled, aiming at gun at Brent. There was a flurry of movement as someone tackled Charlie from behind. A gunshot rang out, something hard punched me and the next thing I knew I was on the floor.

I tried to gather my senses before it all went black.

2 0

The last couple of months had been a blur. I had managed to secure an extension for the assignment from O.W.L. due to personal circumstances, but the new deadline was fast approaching. It seemed like a bizarre lie when I had emailed my tutor to explain that my pyramid-scheme-ruined-step-father had been running dirty money for a woman he barely knew and that while catching her in the act of running an illegal gambling circuit, I had accidentally been shot by a police officer.

If you were a teacher and a student sent that tale to you, you would assume it was an elaborate lie. Fortunately, my tutor and I have met before and she knows exactly how weird my life could be, so she believed me instantly and sent me well wishes for my recovery.

The bullet had grazed my leg, barely a scratch in reality, but it had still been painful and I had dropped to the ground as if I'd been kicked backwards. After blacking out momentarily I woke up to more chaos. There had been a lot of shouting and screaming, mostly from Charlie as he was dragged back up the basement stairs by police, and then Ryan carried me up to the street as we waited for an ambulance.

In my head I had already pictured the dramatic arrival in the emergency room, the doctors ordering every scan, insisting that I be taken straight to theatre for bullet retrieval surgery and that it would all be followed by months of physical therapy to retrain my body so that I *might* walk again. I had been watching a lot of medical dramas just before the whole 'step-dad murder' thing.

In reality someone cleaned the wound and dressed it, then I was sent home. No follow up needed. It had still bought me a delay for the obstacle course task that I had to complete with Quin, which I was grateful for. It had given us more time to 'bond' which looked a lot like me sorting through his receipts at the café and him agreeing not to jump on my head when I was asleep.

One of us was keeping up our end of the bargain.

We also watched each other's favorite movies and talked about them afterwards. After I put 'Mean Girls' on for us to watch, Quin quickly decided that it was now *his* favorite movie of all time and wanted us to work on a choreographed dance routine to a Christmas song for the holidays later in the year. I said I'd think about it.

"Are you ready for this today?" Ryan asked. He had been so tied up with the mountain of admin associated with the Nutraspin case that we hadn't spent much time together since Chessie's arrest. He had promised to take the day off to support me though, and I hadn't realized how much I needed it until he had shown up.

"Yeah, Quin and I made pizza last night and I let him have all the ham, so I think we are in a good place," I laughed.

"The easiest way to his heart *is* through his stomach," Ryan smiled. He was driving us to the obstacle course. It was set up on the grounds of the University of Awa, this meant that I would probably have students and colleagues watching me tumble from great heights as Quin shouted lousy instructions and my blindfolded-self couldn't do a thing about it.

Quin came bounding down the stairs into the hallway, he looked glossy. He had clearly been preening himself all morning in preparation for the big show. I reminded him a few times that this was about *my* studies and that we were working towards *me* getting my full magic license. In the interest of keeping things friendly between us, I didn't remind him again.

"Is that what you're wearing?" Quin asked.

"Quin, I don't know what this obstacle course is going to involve, so I figured workout clothes were the way to go. Should I be wearing high heels and a cocktail dress?" I laughed.

"No, you look… prepared," he purred. Not the confidence boost I needed, but my appearance wasn't important today. I just had to get through the assignment without having a blazing argument with my familiar in front of my tutor, then put this whole thing behind us.

We piled into Ryan's car and began the drive out of Sucré towards the University. I tried to think about *anything* other than the next few hours, like how I was excited that my mom was coming to visit again this weekend. How we had plans to visit a spa and go out for pasta and drink wine.

Since everything happened, she had been finding out more and more snippets of information about Lee's financial problems and the lengths he had gone to so that she never found out. Ryan had helped to recover some of her money that Lee had squandered into Nutraspin, and she was beginning to have more and more good days. I was happy for her, things were starting to feel 'normal' again. It also helped that I was paying for her to get online therapy sessions, she said that was more helpful than any glass of wine ever could be.

Maybe I should focus on something totally unrelated to Sucré. I could ponder all the spare time I would have once my O.W.L. studies were completed, or a fun vacation spot that Ryan and I could visit. Ideally we could have one vacation in our relationship that didn't involve a dead body or a murder investigation.

I pictured white sands and clear blue waters, so lost in the daydream that I didn't realize we had arrived until the engine fell silent.

"Ready?" Ryan asked us both. Quin had fallen asleep on the back seat of the car and my mind was still a thousand miles away in French Polynesia. I wasn't feeling confident.

I woke Quin and carried him across the grass to the obstacle course area. It was all obscured by a large wooden fence. I had been warned about this, it was to stop me memorizing the route and cheating my way to a victory.

Professor Eastey emerged from a door in the fence, carrying a blindfold in one hand and a powdered donut in the other. I assumed only one of those things was for me, and I was right.

"Good to see you again, Nora. Are you feeling up to the challenge?" she asked. My tutor was as weird as she was wonderful, her hair was now a vibrant shade of purple, all tucked under a wool hat but a few strands hung loose. It was a chilly day, but I figured I would soon warm up as I began to navigate my way around the place with only Quin's words for guidance. The thought of it was already making me feel sweaty.

Ryan offered to fasten the blindfold on and Professor Eastey allowed him to guide me to the start of the course. It is so strange to walk over uneven ground without the ability to see. My eyes were closed underneath the black fabric and my stride had shortened to almost a shuffle, I was so sure I would trip and fall if I walked any faster.

"This is where I leave you," Ryan whispered in my ear. He kissed me on the cheek and then I was alone. Someone had decided that Quin required a battery powered microphone to amplify his voice across the field. I already knew that those people would regret it as soon as Quin started talking.

"Nora! Nora! Can you hear me? Nora! Nora? Put both arms in the air if you can hear me!" he yelled.

"Quin, I can speak you know. I can just tell you that I can hear you," I laughed.

"Okay, so you need to turn to the right. Not that much. Imagine you are standing in the middle of a clock and it's like, I don't know, it's noon. Right? So you are facing twelve, but you need to be facing eleven," he said. Wow, that almost made sense. I turned a few degrees to the left. "Perfect, now take a step forward. Now another."

There was movement ahead and when it was combined with the whirring sound, I guessed that something large was spinning. I had seen all those ultimate warrior-type competitions where they had to jump over a spinning beam, or duck under one. Unlike those contestants I was completely blind.

"Nora, drop to the floor!" Quin shouted. I immediately obeyed, feeling a beam miss me by inches as it spun over my body. "Stand up quickly, you are on a narrow walkway so put one foot directly in front of the other as you move, that's right, get ready to jump, now!"

I let out a sigh of relief as I landed safely back onto the walkway. To give credit where credit was due, Quin was giving very clear instructions. I hadn't been entirely sure what the point of this whole exercise was, but seeing him work like this, how competent he can be when he put his mind to it, it made me feel confident in calling on him as my familiar when I needed help.

I must have been halfway up the rope ladder before I remembered that I wasn't fond of heights. Not being able to see how high above the ground I was sure did help, but Quin's voice felt as though it was getting further away quickly. How much more climbing would there be?

"Okay, you are almost at the end now, there is just a huge metal slide at the top and you are going to get in and ride it all the way down to the ground. Yeah... pull yourself up onto that platform, crawl forward, that's it. That's the top of the slide, so climb in so that you are seated at the top and then hold yourself steady until I say so," Quin instructed.

I waited for him to tell me to go, but he was waiting for something. What was there? What threat was lurking in this tunnel that he was trying to protect me from? He hadn't led me wrong so far and I had no reason to doubt him now.

"Now!" he yelled. I let go of the edges and began to slide downwards, my body moving up to the sides as I went around corners. Swirling down and down for what felt like an age. How high up had I been? Through the blindfold I could start to see light, there was an end to the tunnel after all. I rushed out into the open air and landed on a padded floor. Someone was waiting there to lift me up onto my feet.

"You can take your blindfold off now," Quin instructed.

I removed the fabric from my eyes and saw who had lifted me onto my feet. It was the man that was now on one knee in front of me. Ryan.

"Oh my.. I... Ryan," I stuttered. I had my hands covering my mouth in complete shock, struggling to believe that this was happening. He was smiling at me and his eyes sparkled as he watched my reaction. He held up a velvet box.

"I could hardly let you use your magic to predict what was going to happen, so I had to make sure you were suitably distracted," he smirked. I looked around to see that the platform I had landed on was surrounded by huge vases of flowers, the sunlight wrestling through the petals in golden stripes to cast floral shadows on the ground.

"Is Quin in on this?" I asked.

"Of course," Ryan smiled. I looked over to see Quin settling into a seated position near some roses. This was probably the only time Quin had ever kept a secret, I was blown away. "Nora, I am in love with you. There is no one else I want to spend all of my days with. One of the first times we met, you accused me of murder *and* trying to run you off the road. Even as you were yelling at me, I couldn't help thinking that I'd rather argue with you than with anyone," he smiled. "Will you marry me?"

A tear rolled down my cheek and he opened up the velvet box to reveal the most stunning diamond ring I had ever seen in my life. "Yes!" I said, bending down to wrap my arms around him before he had the chance to stand. He squeezed me back, then leaned away so that he could slip the ring onto my finger.

As we kissed, I could hear applause and, glancing with one eye, I realized that my mom and some of my colleagues were approaching us, champagne in hand. We began to float above the ground, as if the happiness of the moment alone was causing us to ascend.

I was surrounded by everything I could ever have wanted and I couldn't believe my luck. Ryan laced his fingers through mind and lifted our hands up to the sky in celebration.

THANKS FOR READING

Thanks for reading, I hope you enjoyed the book. It would really help me out if you could leave an honest review with your thoughts and rating on Amazon. Every bit of feedback helps!

MAILING LIST

Want to be notified when I release my latest book? Join my mailing list. It's for new releases only. No spam.

http://eepurl.com/gIHYJj